Temporary Agency

Also by Rachel Pollack

Golden Vanity
Alqua Dreams
Salvador Dali's Tarot
A Practical Guide to Fortune Telling
78 Degrees of Wisdom
Unquenchable Fire
Tarot Readings and Meditations
The New Tarot
The Haindl Tarot
Shining Woman Tarot
Burning Sky

As Editor

Tarot Tales (co-edited with Caitlin Mathews)

Temporary Agency

Rachel Pollack

St. Martin's Press
New York

ISBN 0-312-11077-4

First published in Great Britain by Orbit.

For Rachel Crosby

'I know an antidote more mighty than the woodcutters and I know a fine preventative against malignant attacks.'

Homer, 'Hymn to Demeter'

Part One

TEMPORARY AGENCY

1

When I was fourteen, a cousin of mine angered a Malignant One. It was a big case, a genuine scandal. Maybe you remember it. At the time, when it all ended, I just wanted to forget about the whole thing. But a couple of years have passed and I guess maybe it's time to think about it again.

The Bright Being lived in the office building where my cousin Paul worked analyzing retail sales reports. I don't know how she got there, really. We never did find that out. I don't even know how long she was there. I mean, before Paul met her. Maybe she lived on that same spot long before the building went up. Maybe she even lived there for thousands of years, way before the Indians came. No one really knows how old the Beings are. Some people say – I read this in a book, actually – that the Bright Beings, the Malignant Ones and the Benign Ones, go back to the beginning of the universe. According to this Sacred Physics book, the Big Bang Story that broke open the cosmic ylem egg showered out the Beings along with all the quarks and tachyons and all the rest of them. The Beings came from a kind of impurity in the ylem, a sort of aesthetic flaw in the original story. So maybe the Ferocious One lived at that spot for millions of years, embedded in the granite of Manhattan Island, waiting for humans, for victims – like my poor cousin Paul.

Or maybe she never lived there at all until the building

went up. Maybe the contractor summoned her, maybe he offered her space in her building in exchange for help in getting his contract bid accepted. I thought of this because of what happened later. And because of what happened with the Defense Department.

Even if you don't remember Paul's case, you'll certainly remember the Pentagon scandal. How half the Defense Department turned out to be Malignant Ones and the other half paying them off. How a lot of people said the chairman of the joint chiefs himself was a Malignant One. That one never made it into the papers, but everyone heard about it.

And you probably remember Alison Birkett. It was the Pentagon scandal that made her famous, after all. Before that she was an unknown lawyer specializing in demonic possession. But then that peace group came to her with their suspicions of 'preternatural harassment', and she began to investigate, and to push. And she kept on investigating, and pushing, for something like five years, until suddenly the story was all over the papers and the TV, and everyone wanted to interview and photograph Alison Birkett. Remember the *Time* magazine cover? They shot her standing on the steps of the Supreme Court, wearing a sharp suit, with the wind blowing a few strands of hair across her face, and the word 'Demonbreaker' slashed across the bottom of the page.

I was just a kid then, but somehow Alison Birkett seemed really special to me. I watched the news every night on TV, hoping to see a feature about her. When one of the networks promised a special hour-long interview with her I begged my parents to let me stay up late that night. And I cut out the picture from *Time* and got a glass frame to preserve it and hang it over my desk.

I followed the scandal more closely than most adults, every detail. I still remember all the excitement, the new charges coming out every day in the paper. I remember the demonstrations, the peace groups in their rainbow robes and animal masks, chanting and waving those orange streamers in huge figure 8s as they marched on the Pentagon. And I remember the incredible excitement when the president ordered the Spiritual Development Agency to drive out the Ferocious Ones. They came in procession, with their twelve-foot banners and fluorescent masks, their drums and bells and electronic trumpets.

I was just a kid. I'd never seen anything like it. We all got off school, just like it was a national sacred-day, and I remember sitting in front of the TV all day long, watching 'the big circus', as my father called it. My mother went nuts trying to get me to eat, especially when they drew those huge lines out from the corners of the building, changing the Penta*gon* to a giant Penta*gram*. Wow, I thought, this is it, now it's going to happen. And I was right, too. The TV blanked out the sound so we couldn't hear the actual formulas the SDA chanted, but we could see the electric fire in the air as the Beings left the walls, only to get trapped in the triangles drawn on the outside of the building. And then when they did the banishment, and erased the lines, and declared the Pentagon 'free and liberated', I cheered and screamed and bounced up and down on the rug in front of the TV.

And I'll never forget my father then, how much he shocked me when he said, 'Oh, sure, right. And just in time for the commercials.'

'What do you mean?' I asked.

'Listen, Honey,' Daddy said, 'our beloved Spiritual Development Agency puts on a good show, but don't you believe everything they say.'

'Mike!' my mother shouted at him. 'She's only a child.'

I guess he realized he'd given me a little more cynicism than I could handle because he said to me, 'I'm sorry, Sweetheart. Your daddy's just shooting off his mouth.'

But the damage was done. 'You're lying,' I screamed at

him, and ran upstairs to my bedroom. There I took down the picture of Alison Birkett and looked at it while I cried. For a few seconds I hugged it, but then that seemed kind of dumb so I put it back on the wall.

I thought about all that stuff after everything that happened with Paul. I thought about the Pentagon, the things my father had said – and something else. Maybe if I'd done things differently, I could have helped Paul, really helped him. Maybe if I hadn't been so trusting, if I'd acted early enough, I could have really done something. Maybe if I'd remembered what my father had said, I wouldn't have expected the SDA to take care of us. I was only fourteen, remember. You can make yourself feel pretty guilty when you're fourteen.

Of course, none of us knew anything at all about this when Paul went to work at that building. And when he met that – *woman* – and got involved with her, he never suspected she was anything different than what she seemed. I mean, you hear about such things happening but you never think it's going to happen to you. Romance with a Bright Being? Come on. It sounds like something out of supermarket magazines, right? 'I lost my husband to a Malignant One', or 'Movie star's new boyfriend a Ferocious One! Details inside!'

Maybe Paul should have guessed something, or at least been a little more careful. Because he did get a warning. When he first got the job he went to a Speaker for a divination. He went to a Bead Woman actually, one of those women who use coloured beads to make their predictions. He took me along. Paul and I were really close, despite his being ten years older than me. We were each an only child and we kind of thought of each other as brother and sister, especially after Paul's folks died in a car crash during his last year of college.

So we went to this Bead Woman who said her blessings and threw out her beads on a silk scarf. Right in the centre lay a red bead with yellow bands, and all around it lay a circle of little black ones. And all the others had scattered to the edges of the cloth. Danger, the Speaker said. Danger and isolation. Paul asked what kind of danger, but she said she couldn't tell because all the other beads had 'retreated'. They talked about it and then Paul decided that since he'd asked about work it had to mean danger at his new job.

So Paul decided to do an environmental enactment for his workplace. I helped him. It was fun. We went down to the big spiritual supply centre on 34th Street and got some sacred paper (made from old clothes worn by the major New York storytellers), and some sanctified chalk and some great miniature office furniture (I loved the little fax machine; it was so cute), and some little plastic dolls to signify Paul and his co-workers, and finally a package of official SDA flash powder. Then we went downtown to Paul's studio in the Village where he had what has got to be the smallest sanctuary you've ever seen (growing up in the suburbs can be pretty boring, but at least the houses all have decent-sized sanctuaries). We drew a circle on the floor for sacred ground and set up the office inside it. Then we labelled one of the dolls with Paul's boss's name and just wrote 'co-worker' on the others, and set them out. Next we took the biggest doll and wrote Paul's name on it, including his official enactment name. While Paul marched the doll into the circle I moved the other dolls back and forth, as if they were all happy and excited about Paul's joining the company. After that, we sang songs of harmony and success while Paul wrote out a few 'positive realities' on the sacred paper. Paul burned the paper on a silver enactment tray and then scattered the ashes on the dolls at their miniature computer desks. Finally, we sang a couple more songs, general all-purpose praise stuff, while we set off the flash powder in the silver bowl that went with the tray. And then Paul took me down to Chinatown for dim sum.

Well, we certainly had fun. And maybe it would have

worked – if the danger had been coming from his office. But in fact it came from another office entirely, one down the hall near the restrooms.

Later on, the SDA questioned Paul pretty heavily about his early encounters with the Being. I'm sure they were trying to get themselves off the hook, in case we decided to go public after all about what she was doing there. And who her clients were. But Paul didn't know or suspect anything when he first saw her. Why should he? As far as he knew, she ran a temp agency. He only went past her office at all because it was on the way to the men's room. In fact, most of the time when he went past it the office was closed. And the few times the door stood open he just saw her on the phone, or entering stuff into a computer. He did notice her. But all he saw was a beautiful woman – long wavy red hair, smooth curves, violet eyes. She wore suits most of the time, he said, kind of severe no-nonsense, with skirts just above the knee.

Paul noticed her and so did all the other guys in his office. But as far as he could tell she took no notice at all of him or any of the others. Some of them called her 'the Ice Queen'. (Why couldn't she have decided to melt for one of them instead of my cousin Paul?) A couple of times, he said, he tried speaking to her at the elevator but never got anywhere. Once, he said, he was standing outside her open office (he didn't say what he was doing there) when her phone rang, and after she'd answered it she got up and went over to close the door. Paul said when he saw her the next day in the lobby he felt himself blush but she just walked right past him.

So what changed her? What made her suddenly go after him, of all the men who worked there? Paul was always vague about this with me, sometimes saying he had no idea, other times hinting he knew something, but didn't think it was important. I'll have to guess, but I do have an idea.

What I guess is that Paul did something which made

him more attractive. I think he did one of the forbidden enactments. Now, I don't mean anything really nasty. Paul would never do anything violent. But just before the Being got interested in him, Paul went on a holiday – a hunting trip, he said. A packaged tour. And he got nervous whenever I tried asking for details. That wasn't like Paul. From around when I was twelve he would always tell me pretty much everything. So I think he went off to one of those 'lodges' men go to, and I think he did something a little more serious than dolls and tiny office furniture. Something with a vow of secrecy, and maybe a couple of 'service' women wearing nothing but body paint and soft furry animal skins.

Men do these things to increase their potency. That's what the magazines say, anyway. Whatever Paul did, it sure got the attention of the 'lady' down the hall. He walked past her office one day just after his trip. She was writing on a chart or something, Paul said, when suddenly she stopped, put down her pencil and looked up at him. Directly at him. She looked curious, he told me, as if she was seeing some interesting animal she'd never encountered before. I remember he laughed when he told me this, just a few days after it happened. Of course, that was before he knew what she was. But I didn't laugh with him. It gave me the creeps, even then.

Paul said he was so startled he almost ran away. Instead, he did his best to smile at her, but she was already back at her work. So he forgot about her until that afternoon when he was waiting for the elevator to go home. He was just standing there, feeling tired, when he heard a voice behind him. The funny thing is, he never remembered what the voice said, just the way it made him feel. He found himself closing his eyes and smiling, and swaying back and forth slightly as if he was balancing himself against a strong wind. He opened his eyes and turned around, and there she was. She had her blazer draped over her arm and she was wearing a satiny blouse, pink,

Paul said it was, and I bet it was open pretty far down, but Paul didn't say that.

In fact, when he first told me about this fantastic woman he'd met he sounded so gushy I should have suspected something just from that. He told me how she touched his arm and all the tiredness left him, how it was like sitting on the grass and watching the river go by. Paul never talked about girls like that. Paul never talked about anything like that.

They went out for a drink, then dinner, to some place Lisa knew. That was the name she used, Lisa. Lisa Blackwell. Goddamn her.

When they said goodnight they kissed, and even though it went on for a while that's all they did. And then she smiled at him, 'like a kid' Paul said, 'like she was younger than you', ('Thanks a lot' I told him, but he paid no attention) and it was okay, he said, it was okay they didn't go any further, because he knew they would do so, maybe the next time or the time after.

I said, 'You better make sure she gets a little older first', but Paul was unstoppable. He just wanted to go on about how okay it all was.

They slept together a few nights later. The SDA investigators made a big fuss about this. Paul told me they asked him over and over what it felt like, didn't he suspect anything? He just kept repeating to them that it was like sleeping with an ordinary woman. That wasn't what he told me. At the time he went on and on with one soupy description after another. He even told me how he prayed that when I started sleeping with boys I would find something so perfect. I said, 'Maybe you and Lisa can coach us.' But he was beyond sarcasm.

If Paul's ga-ga language didn't make me suspicious something else should have. He didn't want me to meet her. Now, I didn't meet all of Paul's girlfriends. I mean, it wasn't like he submitted them to me for approval. But usually, whenever he got serious about someone he'd invite me for lunch or something, so we could all get to know each other. With Lisa he got all evasive whenever I asked to meet her. I don't think he knew he was doing it. He kept saying how he'd told Lisa all about me and how she couldn't wait to meet me. But it never worked out. He would promise, but always 'next week', or after a sales conference, or an out of town trip.

Finally, we did make a date. Paul and Lisa invited me to go with them to the Summer Drum ceremony in Central Park. I don't know how many people reading this have ever been to the Central Park Drum. Most towns have a Summer Drum, but not like this one. Over one hundred thousand people come, many after days of deep mud retreats, so that all they're wearing is globs of dried dirt. People dance, sometimes on one leg, people fly the most amazing kites (some nine levels high, each with its own guardian spirit), people throw sanctified Frisbees painted over with patterns of perfection, groups of three hundred people or more go deep travelling in meditation together, people lie on the grass and hum for hours . . . And then there are the drums, as many as seven thousand of them. The first time Paul took me I thought we'd all bounce up into the sky when the drums started.

Paul and I considered the Central Park Drum something special between the two of us (maybe because we had to fight so hard the first time to get my parents to let me go). When the second Thursday in June approached and Paul just talked about Lisa, Lisa, Lisa, I really felt like he just wanted to get rid of me. So it relieved me when he called to make a date to meet him and Lisa at Founder's Circle on 59th Street before the start of the ceremony.

The thing is, I never made it. My mom drove me to the train station and I waited there, holding my little travelling enactment bag so I could join in with the collective part of the ceremony. And I waited. I waited ten minutes, twenty minutes, half an hour, with all the commuters muttering about last straws, and robber baron prices, and the other drum followers checking their watches and saying blessings, until finally a garbled loudspeaker voice told us the train was cancelled. Fire on the tracks. Next train in two hours. Maybe. I called my mom and she offered to drive me into the city. I thanked her about twenty times, calling her 'a true hero of the revolution'. She laughed and said she'd be right there.

Forty minutes later, she pulled into the train station. Roadblocks all up and down the highway, she said. Industrial action by the State Police who didn't like the state budget crunch taking away their paid personal enactment days. So finally we set out, and in five minutes we had a flat tyre. No problem, I assured my mother, I'd done tyre changing in preparation-for-driving class. With Mom worrying about me getting my good enactment dress dirty I did the tyre a little more slowly than I would have liked, but then it was finished. Off again. Mom said she'd get the tyre fixed after she dropped me off.

We got onto the highway. Clunk, clunk – another flat tyre. So that was it for my trip to meet Lisa Blackwell. By the time the AAA towed us to a gas station and did a purification ceremony on the car, I knew Paul and Lisa would be lost among the hundred thousand.

That night, when I called Paul, he sounded relieved. He denied it when I told him, but I was sure I was right.

He began to look different. His weight went up and down. Sometimes he'd look as skinny as the star of a hunger enactment. Other times he looked all puffed up, like he'd eaten nothing but doughnuts for a month. I even asked him if he was bulimic. He claimed his weight hadn't changed in two years. One time he came to my house for dinner and I got the strangest feeling, like he was fading away, like I could almost see the wall right through him.

His behaviour changed too. Nothing really wild. But he talked a lot. Paul always used to keep silent, especially at family parties. Now he made himself the centre of attention, telling jokes, spouting political theories, giving advice on the economy. And he bragged. Paul never bragged about himself, but now he was telling us all about his two promotions in two months, his special commendation from the CEO, even how much he spent for a new suit. I wanted to scream at him. Or kick him.

My folks didn't notice anything. They just said wasn't it great Paul was coming out of his shell? Wasn't it wonderful he was doing so well? And in such a short time. And didn't Lisa sound sweet?

How could we have been so damn stupid? He even told us how Lisa – wonderful sweet Lisa – had received a vision of Paul going all the way to the top. As if she'd done a 'selfless offering' and the Powers had granted her a psychic vision. Damn. If only we'd gotten the fog out of our heads maybe we could have intervened.

But it was up to Paul to recognize that something was wrong. He started getting strange dreams. There were lots of lights, he told me later, glowing on the sides of buildings, swooping down out of the skies, flaring up in front of his face. And when he'd put his hands up or made a noise he'd hear laughter. Except he wouldn't see anybody. Other dreams, instead of lights he'd see holes. Holes in walls, in the street, in stores and lobbies of buildings. And nobody would see them but him. In the dream Paul would point out the holes to people. 'Watch out,' he'd say to an old woman, 'you're going to step in that hole.' But instead of looking, they'd just shove him out of the way. Sometimes holes would appear in people's bodies. In the dream he'd go over to examine them, sometimes even reach inside their bodies and find nothing but garbage. He'd call people over to help, but they'd all just laugh. A few times, Paul told me later, he woke up from these dreams feverish or even vomiting.

I asked Paul if he ever took the dreams to NORA, the computer for the National Oneiric Registration Agency. No, he said, once he woke up, he'd just wanted to forget about them. I asked him if he'd done enactments to cleanse his dream spirit. No, he told me, and looked surprised. He'd never thought about it.

Even awake, he started acting funny. If he didn't see Lisa he just stayed home and did nothing, not even watch TV. He stopped seeing his friends, he stopped seeing me. He started getting scared at really odd moments. He'd see a bus pulling up to a kerb and suddenly panic as the door opened. As if a wild dog or something would come leaping out at him.

But what really worried him finally was Lisa herself. She never tired. At first, he liked that. 'She can go on and on,' he said to me once, before it started to scare him. When he was with her he never got tired, either. They could make love four or five times, he told me, something he said he could never do with anyone else. 'It's almost like inflight refuelling,' he said. Of course, he was bragging again. And yet – I don't think he realized this – he became all sad after he said it. We were drinking tea and I remember he stared into the cup like an old-fashioned Speaker looking for a message in the leaves.

Finally, he would fall asleep and dream his strange dreams. He always figured Lisa was asleep too, until one night he woke up in the middle of the night and she was just lying there, wide awake, staring at the ceiling, and smiling. When she turned and reached for him he jumped back. He had to go pee, he told her. She laughed. In the bathroom, he said, he thought his heart would punch right through his chest. He didn't know why, he said, he just felt so scared. But then she called him and suddenly he found himself excited. You know, aroused. He told me it was like his 'thing' had gotten a life of its own and was running away with him.

After that, Paul tried to pull back from her, see her less, stay home, go out with friends. Nothing worked. I don't mean he lost control, like some sort of drug fiend, or found himself calling her and hating himself for doing it. No, I mean he couldn't stay away. He literally couldn't. He would sit down, alone, in front of the TV with a rental movie on the VCR. He'd even put on pyjamas and get into bed. And then suddenly he'd find himself ringing her bell, with only the slightest memory of getting dressed, leaving the house with the TV still running, and getting a cab to 79th Street where Lisa lived. Or else he'd go to a bar with some friends, tell jokes and drink for half an hour, then excuse himself as if he was going to the men's room, and instead just leave and go uptown to Lisa's.

For a while he thought – he tried to think – it was an ordinary obsession. He even went to one of those groups for 'love addicts' where they do enactments to purify their bodies and ask their higher powers to shield them from the lower powers. But when the others talked of their need for reassurance because their parents had never loved them, or described the thousands of dollars they'd spent at singles' retreats, Paul knew his problem came from another level.

He kept thinking he should do something, maybe a freedom enactment. But he could never seem to do it. He would plan one, set up his sanctuary with strings of flowers and twenty-four-hour candles, spray the air with purifier, and go off to work, determined to go home right away and fulfil the inner path, as people say. Instead, he'd let Lisa take him off to a disco and then her apartment, and by the time he'd get home, the candles would have burned out and flower petals would lie all over the floor.

One time he tied his childhood spirit string around his wrist when he went to work. Since Paul's parents' death the string had meant a lot to him. He used to keep it in a special glass case on his permanent altar. When he put it on that day, his wrist stung for a moment and he found he wanted to yank it off and throw it away. Instead, he left it on, and suddenly the pain vanished and he closed his eyes and smiled. He went to work, he told me later, more cheerful than he'd felt in weeks. At lunchtime when he saw

Lisa she 'twitched' (his word) when he kissed her. That night, when they made love, she said she wanted to play and gave him some kind of costume to wear (he wouldn't say what). Only, he had to take everything off, including the string. The next morning when he got dressed he couldn't find it. They searched the whole bedroom, until Lisa persuaded him he better get to work. She'd give it to him when she found it, she said. Sure.

And then, one night, Lisa had some kind of appointment. So Paul stayed home for once and was watching *Slade!*, that cop show on TV where the hero investigates possession for the SDA. In the episode, Slade goes to a Southern town to investigate some mysterious deaths and gets stonewalled by the local sheriff's office. At one point, a woman is running through a swamp, trying to escape a group of Malignant Ones who've taken the form of dogs and cats. She takes refuge in a cabin and bars the door. Inside, she recites the Standard Formula of Recognition. You know, 'Ferocious One, I beg you to release me. I know that nothing I have done deserves your Malignant Intervention.' Well, in the story, she gets halfway through the formula when one of the dogs smashes through the door and knocks her to the ground. Then, after they all attack her, they change into the local cops. Shock. Horror. Commercial.

But for Paul the real shock came with his reaction to the Formula. Without realizing it, he started to say it out loud in his apartment. He got as far as 'Ferocious One, I beg you to release me. I know—' And then he stopped, gasping in pain. He felt, he said, like someone had kicked him in the stomach. When he stopped speaking the pain eased, but he was shaking and sweating. A couple of minutes later, he thought of trying it again, but just the thought filled him with terror. The panic stopped as soon as he gave up the idea of trying to say the Formula.

Paul didn't sleep much that night. He just lay in bed, wondering if he should call the SDA emergency number, telling himself it could wait until morning, jumping every time he heard a strange noise outside his apartment or even the wind against his window. Over and over again he thought how if he wasn't saying the Formula he should do something else, maybe set up a ring of protection, or else just write down his fears on sanctified paper and burn them. Instead, he just lay in bed, terrified. But when morning came, it all seemed okay again. Paul found himself laughing at his 'paranoia'. His suggestiveness. He shouldn't watch so much TV, he told himself.

Two days later, however, he managed to tell Lisa he was sick and was going to leave work early. Come to her office, she told him. She could make him feel better. Heal him. Her friends told her she was a natural healer. She had healing hands, they said. Her friends said she should quit her temp agency and run a hand sanctuary.

Paul realized he had never met Lisa's friends. Not a single one. Nor her family. He started to feel clammy and cold, and thought how he didn't need to lie to go home sick.

He left his office but he didn't go home. Instead, he changed his suit for jeans, T-shirt, dark glasses and cap, and sat in a diner across the street from the building. When Lisa left he followed her. At first, he tried to stay close to the buildings, even duck into doorways. But after a couple of minutes, when she didn't look back, he got bolder, even moved up close. This is ridiculous, he told himself. If she did spot him, she probably would just laugh at him. Never let him forget it. Maybe he could convince her it was some sort of sex game. He half felt that way himself. He would get aroused and instead of him following her, it felt like Lisa had hold of his penis, like a tow rope, and was pulling him along (his image, not mine).

He followed her to a hospital, the huge Mirando Glowwood Sanctuary for the Healing Arts on 7th Avenue. Paul expected they would need passes to go up to the rooms, but no one seemed to take any notice of either of them as he followed her past the front desk to the giftshop, where she bought a mixed bouquet of flowers, and then up a couple of flights of stairs. Paul found himself relaxing. After all his suspicions, she was just visiting a sick friend.

Paul never found out what was wrong with the man in room 603. He was so concerned that no one give him away he didn't even bother to notice if the floor focused on any special area of medicine. When Lisa entered the room Paul strolled past the doorway, slow enough to notice a man asleep or unconscious in a private room, with a man and woman in chairs beside the bed. Friends of Lisa, he thought, with a guilty thrill that he finally could meet some of her friends if only he could think up an explanation for how he got there. But then the man and woman just got up and left, seemingly without even noticing Lisa was in the room. Paul pretended to be reading the names posted outside a room down the hall until the two had left, and then he moved back to just outside 603, where he could look inside without being noticed.

Lisa had pulled back the sheets and now was unbuttoning the man's pyjamas, all without him moving or opening his eyes. Paul said he looked like he'd been lying there, unconscious, for a long time. There were sores up and down his body. When the man's body lay all exposed, Lisa began to undress. Paul told me how he wanted to run, to get as far away as he could, but he couldn't make himself move.

The moment Lisa straddled the man, he came alive. Or rather his body came alive, thrusting into her and thrashing on the bed. The man himself stayed unconscious, his face as blank, Paul said, as the sky. Nor did anyone else seem to notice anything. The bed thumped, strange noises came out of the man's throat, yet people just walked by – patients in bathrobes, visitors, nurses. Once, a woman in one of those candy-striped volunteer outfits bumped

into Paul, smiled cheerfully and walked on, taking no
notice either of the pounding noises inside the room or
Paul staring back at her terrified.

As the body rolled about with Lisa the sores opened
up, spitting out a thick mixture of blood and pus, like a
fountain with ten or twenty spouts. Paul watched it soak
the bed, ooze down onto the floor. He watched Lisa scoop
it up in her hands and smear it all about the man's face.
She's killing him, he thought, and knew he should run for
help, or at least cry out. But he just stayed and watched.

When Lisa finally lifted off the man, he went limp
again, draped across the drenched bed. Only now Lisa
took the flowers she'd bought and placed them on the
man's genitals, where they – clung. That was the word
Paul used. The flowers seized the man's crotch like some
animal feeding on his discharges.

Despite everything, Paul said, he was sure he didn't
make any noise. He didn't gag, or shout, or anything.
Lisa just stood there, naked, with her back to him and
said, in a friendly voice, 'How was that, Paul? Was it
what you expected? Was it scary enough? Or should
I have laid rats on him instead of flowers? I could
still do that if you like. I just thought this might be
more fun.'

Paul wanted to run, but he couldn't. He could hardly
stand upright as Lisa turned and came towards him.
'Ferocious One,' he managed to say, 'I beg you—'

Lisa laughed. 'Paul, Paul,' she said, 'it's much too late
for that. And why would you want to send me away?
Haven't I told you I love you? Didn't I promise to make
you rich?'

'Promise?' Paul said.

'Go to work next morning. My intuition tells me your
boss wants to send you on a management training course.'
She stepped towards him.

'No!' Paul shouted, and then he did jump back, out
of the doorway. Finally, people were looking at him. A

man on crutches stopped to stare. Paul said, 'I never . . .
I thought they just—'

'Oh, Paul. You don't really think you got all those
promotions by your own talents, do you? Trust me,
darling. Let me take care of you. Let me help you.'

Now Paul ran. Pushing people out of the way, he hurtled
down the stairs and out of the lobby into the street. He
ran as hard as he could, pumping his arms like you see on
TV (I can see him, with his cap and dark glasses, and his
mouth gulping for air. Poor Paul. Poor dumb Paul).

A few blocks down he dared to turn around. Lisa wasn't
following. At least he didn't see her. Maybe she'd taken
some other form. Maybe she'd disguised herself as an old
woman walking on the other side of the street. Or a cat
sitting on a stoop. Or a car parked illegally in front of
a pump. What did he know, after all, about Malignant
Ones and their powers? It's the kind of thing you learn in
school, fourth grade sacred studies class, and then forget
right after the test.

When he saw a cab, he started to hail it, then stopped.
What was an empty cab doing in midtown at that time
of day? Maybe that Russian-looking cab driver was Lisa.
Or another Malignant One coming to her aid. But maybe
it was a *Benign* One. A Devoted Being who had noticed
Paul's danger and jumped in its taxi to come to his rescue.
How could he know? How could he know? How could he
tell the difference? He took the bus.

Crammed in with shoppers and office workers, Paul
wished he could just close his eyes, let the crowd hold
him up, and sleep. Finally he made it to his apartment
building and the fear hit him all over again. Lisa had a
key. Lisa didn't need a key. She probably could fade right
through a closed window. But if he didn't go in, where
could he go? How could he live? He told me later he
imagined himself lying in some corner outside the men's
room in Grand Central Station.

When he told me all this, he stopped at that point in

the story. 'What happened?' I said. 'Did you go inside? What did you do?' He wouldn't look at me and I knew he'd done something he thought was terrible. Finally he confessed. He said he went to the super and told him he'd smelled gas before and was nervous to go back in, and would the super check for him and wave out the window if everything was all right? 'I gave him ten bucks,' Paul said. 'Can you believe it? Ten bucks and maybe that thing would be there waiting for him?'

'But it's okay,' I told him. 'She wasn't there. So he ended up with ten dollars for doing nothing.'

'I guess so,' Paul said. I'd never seen him look so low.

'And you got here safely,' I reminded him.

'Right. So now you're in danger too.'

'Come on,' I said. 'All we've got to do is figure out how to get rid of her.' I almost blushed, knowing how dumb that sounded.

When Paul got inside, he said, he ran all around, checking the bathroom, the closets, even the small cabinets under the bathroom sink. He didn't know what he was looking for, he just had to look. What could he do, he thought, what could he do? I imagined him standing there, outside that tiny sanctuary of his, maybe hitting his hand against his forehead.

While he was trying to figure out what to do next, the phone rang. Paul reached out, then stopped. When the answering machine came on, he waited through his announcement. And then she was there, telling him cheerfully, 'Silly Paul, why don't you pick up the phone? You know I won't harm you. I've got some wonderful ideas for later in the evening.' Then her voice sharpened. 'Paul! Pick up the phone.'

Paul told me later that he had no idea how he managed to resist. His hand moved out to the phone, he stood there almost touching it, his hand shaking. He probably would have picked it up if the doorbell hadn't rung. He jerked his hand back and ran to the door. The super stood there, looking confused. 'Sorry to bother you,' he told Paul, trying to look over Paul's shoulder. 'What's that?'

The answering machine, Paul told me later, had screeched, as if someone had run a fingernail along the tape.

Paul thanked the super, told him everything was okay, said goodbye – and then asked him please to stay there. While the poor confused man stood in the doorway, Paul got out his carryon bag and threw in some clothes, his shaving stuff, and the cat's claw he'd gotten during his first winternight initiation.

I've wondered since if the super was really a Devoted One. Isn't that what they do, help you at some crucial moment? No way to know. People always say the Benign Ones lift you gently, the Malignant Ones knock you down with a club. But Paul wasn't thinking about anything like that. He just pulled his stuff together as fast as he could. And called me.

I still feel good about that. He called me, his fourteen-year-old kid cousin. I know I didn't protect him, not in the long run. And I guess he didn't expect me to save him or anything. But he needed help and he called me. I'll always love him for that.

'Ellen!' he said when he got me on the phone. 'Ellen. Oh, my God.'

I said something dumb, like, 'What's wrong?'

'Lisa,' he said, and stopped.

'What is it?' I asked him. 'Is she hurt?' Dumb.

'She's . . . she's not—'

'She's not hurt?'

'She's not human!'

'No!' I said. 'Oh Paul. Oh God.' He didn't have to say the label. I knew. Stupidly, I said, 'Is she there?'

'No. No, of course not. Of course she's not here. She just called . . . I couldn't— What can I do? I tried the Formula. She laughed at me. I got sick the first time. And then she just laughed. Ellen, what am I going to do?'

'Get over here,' I said. 'Where are you?'

'Home. My place.'

'Get out of there. Right now. Come here.'

'I don't want you getting hurt,' Paul said.

'Don't worry about that,' I said. 'I'll protect us.' Brave talk. 'Just get the train. Take a taxi from the station. Ask for Johnny or Bill. Tell them you're my cousin. You got that? Johnny or Bill.'

'Yes.'

'Hurry.'

'Shouldn't I do an enactment?' Paul asked.

'Do a quick one.'

'What should I do? I can't think.'

'Um – do you have flash powder?'

'Yes, of course.'

'Okay,' I said. 'How about that traveller's amulet I gave you that time you went to Europe?'

'It's in my sanctuary.'

'Great. Go put it on.'

Slow seconds passed while I heard Paul moving things around and cursing. Finally he came back on the phone. 'I can't find it,' he said. Panic pushed his voice up. 'She must have taken it.'

'It's all right,' I said. 'Just . . . just sprinkle the powder around the edges of the floor and especially on the threshold. And—' I was thinking fast. 'Write down— take off your shoes and socks and write out— Do you have an SDA body marker?'

'Yes. I think so.'

'Great. If you can't find it, don't worry. A regular pen will do. But use the marker if you can. Write down the Formula for a safe journey and a safe arrival on the bottoms of your feet. Then light the powder—'

'Should I put my shoes back on?'

'Yes, of course. Light the powder on the threshold and at the same time ask the Devoted Ones for help, and then jump over the powder. Have you got that?'

'Yeah,' Paul said.

'Okay. Leave the phone off the hook so I can hear. And when you leave give me a shout so I can hang up my phone.'

It took Paul at least five minutes, during which I could hardly breathe I was so scared I'd hear him scream or something. Finally I heard the hiss of flash powder and then, from a distance, 'Okay, Ellen.'

Softly, I prayed, 'Bless your feet, and bless your hands, and bless your eyes and mouth. Earth move you in safety and joy across Her shiny face. *Go, Paul.*'

I went downstairs, acting calm so my folks wouldn't find out anything and panic. I figured the last thing we needed was my folks getting hysterical. They'd call the police or something, or just start screaming and no one would do anything.

I got a piece of sanctified chalk and some of my own flash powder and matches from my altar and stuck them in my skirt pocket. Then I went to the kitchen for a glass of milk and cookies. Wholesome. A kid getting a snack. I strolled outside and as soon as I was out of sight of my folks I got to work. I walked three times around the house, flicking drops of milk from the glass onto the ground as I prayed to the Hidden Mother for blessings and protection on the house and all our family. Next I crushed the cookies and scattered the crumbs along the flagstones and the driveway and out to the road, calling for Devoted Ones to flock to Paul's aid and lead him safely out of danger to my house. In the street I drew a box for the house and then two stick figures for Paul. One showed him inside the house, holding hands with a smaller stick figure (me). The other showed him outside with a circle around him, protection against a pair of bat-like wings above his head. Lisa. Then I drew dots from the Paul out in the danger place to the one safe in the house. While I made two little piles of flash powder, one on each Paul, I called once more on the Benign Ones to help him, thanking them in advance. 'Devoted Ones, we thank you for your devotion. We know that nothing we have done deserves your precious intervention.' I fired up the flash piles, waited ten seconds, then dashed back inside.

Upstairs in my room I took all my stuffed totem animals and lined them up on the windowsill. 'Take care of him,' I begged them. 'Please guard him now. Please.' I didn't move from that window until I saw Paul step out of the taxi. Then I threw myself downstairs and out the door.

Maybe I should have stayed at the window until he actually got to the house. I don't know. Maybe if he'd made it all the way under his own power he would have stayed safe, with the strength later to fight back. Because maybe something was taking care of him, feeding him, and when I ran out to get him, I drove it away. Or maybe I weakened my own safety enactment by leaving the house. I don't know. When I saw him – he was limping, with his face screwed up, as if he'd twisted his ankle – I filled up with joy and fear at the same time, and just couldn't wait. If I did something wrong, if I made it worse, I hope Paul forgives me.

We told my folks Paul had hurt himself running and needed to sit down in my room while I brought him some tea. When I got Paul alone, and brought up the tea, I opened a fresh can of blessing powder, sprinkled some on his face and then his bad ankle (he fell running for the train), and finally around the edge of the room. And then I had him tell me everything. It was pretty scary. A couple of times, like when he got to the flowers in the hospital, I had to stop him, holding up my hand like a traffic cop until I could catch my breath. When he finished, I hugged him, with my head on his shoulder so he wouldn't see me cry.

I knew I couldn't do that for long. We had to take care of him. We had to get him some real protection. As well as sprinkling some more blessing powder, we touched our amulets together, stuffed our pockets with prayers written on sanctified paper and put Nora and Toby, my two most powerful stuffed totem animals, in their SDA sanctified travelling cases to take with us. Then I called the taxi company and asked them to send Billy right away.

As we headed downstairs, the phone rang. We were almost out the door when my mother called from the living room, 'Paul? It's for you. It's a woman.' You'd think she'd find it confusing that someone would call Paul at her house. But no, her voice sounded like wasn't it wonderful that she could help two such marvellous people get together. Paul started to walk towards her. I stared at him for a moment before I realized what was happening. When I grabbed his arm he almost shook me loose. I held on, though, and hollered to my mother, 'We've got to leave, Mom. Tell her she missed him.'

'Won't that be rude?' my mother said. 'She sounds so sweet.' But I already had Paul out the door, where, thank the powers, Billy was already pulling into the driveway.

That has got to be the scariest trip I have ever taken, worse even than my high school wilderness initiation. Everyone looked like a Malignant one – the driver cutting us off on the Expressway, the traffic cop halting our lane, the boy roaring past on his motorcycle, even the bag lady sleeping on the sidewalk outside the Nassau headquarters of the SDA.

We told the secretary we needed to speak to an investigator. 'Urgently,' I said. She sent us to a woman about twenty-five, with large amazed eyes. She wore a red blouse and a cotton jumper and had her hair pulled back with a velvet band. While Paul was talking – he got pretty worked up, waving his arms and trying not to cry, he was so scared – the woman, Julie her name tag said, wrote everything down, constantly telling Paul it was all right, he was safe now. 'Your SDA' would protect him.

After she finished taking down his story she went for her superior, a man about forty or fifty, very businesslike, but still basically friendly. Until he asked Paul where he'd met the Ferocious One. 'I told you,' Paul said, 'at work.'

'Fine,' the man said, 'but where exactly is that?' He

smiled at Julie who looked embarrassed that she hadn't gotten such a basic detail. Paul told him the address. He froze. His pen stopped in mid-air, his head in mid-nod. Finally he looked up at Paul and said, 'And you say she worked in an office?'

'She ran a temp agency,' Paul said.

The man's mouth twitched. 'Just a moment,' he told Paul, and walked off. Looking a little confused, and embarrassed, Julie told Paul again that everything would be fine. About a minute passed and then Julie's boss called her from a doorway. He said, 'Ms Stoner,' instead of Julie. When she left the room he closed the door behind her.

About five minutes later the man came back alone. He said, 'Now then, Mr—' He looked at his clipboard. 'Mr Cabot. Why do you think this woman, this Lisa, is a Malignant One?'

'Think?' Paul said.

I stepped forward. 'Excuse me,' I said. 'What's your name?'

'Please, young lady,' he told me. 'I'm trying to check your—' His voice went up in a question.

'Cousin,' I said.

'Cousin, fine. Your cousin's story.'

'You can check it a lot easier if you tell us your name,' I said.

He sighed. 'John Sebbick.'

I smiled sweetly. 'Thank you.'

'I don't understand,' Paul said to him. 'What do you need to check?'

Sebbick said, 'You must realize, Mr Cabot, we get a great many claims made here. People accuse their co-workers, neighbours—' he smiled, '—lovers all the time.'

'I'm not *accusing* her,' Paul half shouted. 'She's a Ferocious One.'

'So you say.'

'I told you what she did with that sick man. In the hospital.'

'What you say she did.'

'I don't believe this,' Paul said. 'Why won't you believe me?'

'Excuse me,' I said, and smiled as big a smile as that goddamn bureaucrat. 'Mr Sebbick, this man has come to you for help. Isn't that your job? To help him?'

'Young lady,' he said. He looked like he'd pat me on the head if he wasn't afraid I'd bite him. 'The SDA does not need children to tell it its job.'

I wasn't going to let that one stop me. I said, 'What are you going to do for him?'

'We will investigate his story,' he said.

'That's not good enough,' I told him. He looked at me like *I* was a Ferocious One. 'He needs protection,' I said. 'How are you going to protect him?'

Sebbick said, '*We* will determine who needs protection in this case.'

I took Paul's arm. 'Come on,' I said, 'let's get you some real help.' He looked at me, grateful, as if he thought I could beat down the whole SDA. I felt myself blush and turned Paul around before that bastard Sebbick could see.

Outside, Lisa was waiting. I didn't need Paul to introduce us, I knew her immediately. She wore a strange triangular-shaped dress, with wide sharp shoulders and hard narrow hips. Her face shone and her golden hair lifted softly in the breeze. She stood back against a black convertible with its top down. She smiled, and for a moment I walked towards that smile, until I realized what I was doing and stopped myself. Next to me, Paul was shaking.

'Poor sweet Paul,' she said. 'I told you, you don't need to be frightened. I have no plans to harm you.'

'Leave him alone,' I blurted. Great. Really effective.

She looked down at me. She seemed suddenly much taller. The points on her padded shoulders gleamed, like knife blades in the sunshine. She said, sweetly, 'This must be your little cousin. What a lovely child.' Her mouth opened very wide. 'Would you like me to swallow you?'

I felt dizzy, nauseated. My feet slid around, as if I was standing on ice, as if the street would crack open and drop me into freezing water. Somehow, my hand went out and found a parking meter. 'Ferocious One,' I said, and gasped as a pain shot into my side. 'We beg you—' The pain became unbearable, and I knew it would stop if I just stopped talking. I said, 'We beg you to release us.' My side ripped open and I screamed. When I looked down I saw blood and meat pouring out onto the sidewalk. I jerked my eyes away as I forced the final words out. 'We know that nothing we have done deserves your Malignant intervention.' And the pain ended. I gasped in relief, and when I looked down my clothes weren't even torn.

Sometimes the old stuff works better than we know. The Formula comes to us from the Tellers after all, and not the SDA. Lisa pretended not to notice, but she backed away. Laughing, she slid into her open-top car. 'I told you,' she said to Paul, 'you don't need to be afraid of me. I'm on your side. Even the SDA will help you if I tell them to.' She laughed again, and then she looked at me. I held on to the parking meter. She said, 'Goodbye, Ellen Pierson. I'm sure we will meet again.' And then she drove off.

On the way home, Paul decided to tell my folks. Well, they reacted just the way I knew they would – Mom crying and fluttering her arms, Daddy ranting about the SDA and its 'ineffectual posturing'. Only, they added a new twist. They attacked Paul for involving me. 'A mere child,' my mother called me. Cute.

I tried to push them onto what really mattered. 'The SDA's not just ineffectual,' I tried to say. 'They're blocking him. That Sebbick –' I stopped myself saying 'bastard' – 'guy is very effectual. You should have seen the way he smirked at us.' No good. They weren't listening. The whole thing had scared them too much. They talked about the danger to me, but they really meant the danger to themselves as well. 'We've got to do something,' I kept saying, and, 'How can we get protection?' It was only when they suggested Paul 'go home and get some rest' that I realized what was going on. They wanted to get rid of him. They figured if he stayed there in our living room Ferocious Ones would come smashing through the picture window at any moment.

'He's not going anywhere,' I said. I made my voice so calm, so firm, that my father just stared at me.

My mother said, 'But she'll get all of us if he stays here.' When nobody answered her for a second and she realized how that sounded, she added, 'We've got to think of you, Ellen.'

'If we send him away,' I said, 'we'll really expose ourselves to danger.'

'What do you mean?' my mother asked.

I was improvising, trying to pull stuff out from what I remembered from school. I said, 'The Devoted Ones don't like it when humans turn against each other. If we lose the support of the Devoted Ones what'll we do if Lisa decides to attack us just for being Paul's family?'

I could see them wavering. I pushed on. 'At his own place it's already too late. He's already invited her in. Here we can put up a wall of protection. We can get help.' I felt like I was explaining things to two year olds. I just prayed that the Guardian of Inappropriate Speech would stop Paul from saying something dumb, like how he didn't want to make any trouble and maybe he should go home. But he just sat there, bent over, his eyes fixed on the middle of the rug. And finally my folks gave in. Paul could stay, they said, 'at least for a few days'.

I added, 'While we get some help.'

'Right,' my father said, as if he'd thought of it.

As soon as I knew they weren't going to change their minds I told them of the enactment I'd already done and suggested maybe we could do it over, all of us together. Daddy said Paul should stay inside. 'We don't want to tempt anything,' he said, but he just likes to take charge. So we went through the routine, mostly Daddy and I, while Mom followed along behind us.

When we got back inside, my father called his lawyer. I was afraid he might not push it hard enough, but he was great. He shouted at the man, told him he had to get the best person and he had to get him right now.

After my father put down the phone, we all said nothing for a while. No one looked at anybody. I don't know how long we would have stood there like that if we didn't hear a knock at the door. My mother half shrieked, my father said, 'Oh God,' Paul whimpered, and I don't remember what I did. Because we all knew who it was. None of us moved, and then the knock came again, and then Paul started to get up. Now, Malignant Ones can't force their way into a house, at least for the first time, unless they're invited. That much I knew. But Paul was contaminated, and none of us was sure just what that meant.

I ran over to him and grabbed his shoulders and held on. He was sweating or crying or both, because his face was all wet, and I think I was crying too, but I held on to him. Daddy ran up and held him too, and then Mom came and put her arms around all of us and together we said the Formula and then the prayers of protection we'd made up for our enactment. And the knocking stopped.

We stood there a long time, hanging on to each other and shaking like one big animal. And then the phone rang. We all just looked at it, letting it ring on and on, until finally my father picked up the receiver. Before he said anything, he switched on the loudspeakers. 'Hello,' he said, and his voice broke.

A woman's voice sounded in the room. 'This is the office of Alison Birkett,' she said. 'This is a protected line, federal registration no. 7237785. You may speak without fear or danger.'

Oh my God, I thought, *he did it. Daddy did it! He got us Alison Birkett.* The SDA itself had turned against us and none of us had any idea why. But now the woman who'd broken the Pentagon Possession, who had forced the Defense Department to admit its involvement with Malignant Ones, had come to save us. I ran and hugged Paul. 'It's her,' I whispered. 'It's Alison Birkett.'

Not exactly, for the woman said, 'Please hold for Ms Birkett.'

A moment later a firm alto voice came on. 'Good afternoon,' she said. 'May I speak with Mr Michael Pierson?'

'Speaking,' my father said.

'Your lawyer, Mr Athenauer, asked me to call you.'

'Yes,' Daddy said. 'Yes, thank you very much for calling.'

'Perhaps you could tell me the problem,' she said.

We took turns, first Daddy, then Paul, then me. I couldn't believe I was speaking to her. I still had her photo over my desk. She didn't talk down to me, or treat me like a child or anything. She just listened and asked a lot of questions, and afterwards she said, 'You did very well, Ms Pierson. Having the name of the official will help us move much more quickly. Thank you.'

'Thank you too,' I said back.

When Daddy asked what would happen, Ms Birkett said, 'The first thing we need to do is secure your house and your presence on an emergency basis. I'll send my team over. Then we need to discover why the SDA refused to help your nephew. I'm going to file a request under the Freedom of Information Act. Usually these things take months, but I believe I can expedite it. There are ways. With luck, we will know something within two weeks.'

'Two weeks?' my mother said. She sounded like she wanted to run away from home.

Ms Birkett said, 'If nothing else, the request should shake some people up.' I could hear the smile in her voice. After telling us how the team would identify themselves, she said goodbye and hung up. 'Goodbye,'

I said softly, even though I knew she couldn't hear me.

The depossession team arrived half an hour later, two men and a woman, all carrying old-fashioned black doctor bags. They wore one-piece protective suits, heavy-tread boots, insulated gloves and animal head masks. The woman was small, about my height. She wore a crocodile mask and on the groin of her protective suit she'd handpainted a silver circle over two wavy blue lines – the moon of power over the river of continuous birth. I couldn't take my eyes off her.

While they unpacked their equipment, my mother asked, 'Will our house be okay?'

'Oh, we don't anticipate any trouble,' the taller of the two men said. He wore an elephant mask. 'Ms Birkett said this was a prophylactic operation.'

They stayed four hours, measuring, taking readings on the house and on us ('Do we have to undress?' I asked the crocodile lady, but all she did was move a stick up and down my body, like when they check for guns at airports), chanting, sprinkling powders, drawing signs on the doors and windows, filling rainbow-coloured balloons with some kind of gas and then popping them in the air, and finally, spraying the four of us with some sort of mist from an unmarked plastic pump bottle (I asked if they used to use aerosols before the ozone crisis, but the crocodile only grunted). They gave each of us a smaller pump and told us to spray ourselves every time we left the house.

Before they left, the elephant warned us not to allow any strangers into our house. 'No salesmen,' he said, 'no polltakers, no free samples, no meter readers or deliveries of bottled gas or anything like that, no building inspectors, no one. If you need any repairs done make sure you know the person ahead of time. And if you have any friends over, even family, make sure they don't bring over any third parties you've never met before. If they do, simply apologize and don't let them in, no matter how much your friends vouch for them. Do you understand that?' We all nodded. 'Good. Now – this is very important – when people come over that you do know, make them say their names out loud *before* they step over the threshold. Make them say, "My name is blank" before they enter the house. The same goes for anyone who might lean over the windowsill.'

I said, 'We'll keep all the windows closed.'

'Good,' the elephant said.

Mom said, 'Won't it seem kind of strange if we ask people to say that? I mean, if we know them anyway?'

I knew what she meant. They'll know we're possessed. People will talk about us. I said, 'We can tell them we're doing a blessing enactment. They get to take part by saying their names.'

'Good girl,' the elephant said, and the crocodile added, 'You would all do well to listen to this young lady. From what Ms Birkett tells us, she knows what she's doing.' I really had to fight to keep my face straight.

My father asked, 'What about going out?'

'No problem,' the elephant said, 'at least for the three of you. The measures we've taken will effectively seal you against personal intervention. At least if you make sure not to invite her into your house. That's the important thing. For Mr Cabot the situation is a little more touchy. He should stay inside as much as possible.' Paul nodded.

Mom said, 'How long will this go on? We can't live like this forever.'

I can't be sure, but I think the elephant glanced at me before he answered her. 'I'm sure Ms Birkett will take care of it, and then you can resume your normal life.'

'Shouldn't we go see her or something?' I asked.

The crocodile said, 'She'll call you.' And then they wished us good luck, made some sweeping hand signs over our heads – and left.

Paul spoke first, the first real sentence he'd said in hours. 'God, I'm so tired.'

'C'mon,' I said, 'I'll take you upstairs.'

He half turned towards my folks. 'I'm sorry,' he said. 'I'm really sorry.'

'It's okay,' Mom said, and Daddy added, 'We're getting help, that's what matters.'

I was happy to arrange the guest room, to make Paul's bed and get him towels. I was happy to get away from my parents. After I'd set up Paul, I went to my room and took down the photo of Alison Birkett. For quite a while I sat there, holding it in my hands, looking at the way she just stood there, as firm as a tree on the stone steps of the court.

We saw Ms Birkett thirteen days later. Those two weeks were really hard for me. They were hard for everyone, of course, and I guess I was as scared as the others, but I also had to speak to my friends and everyone, and not tell them what had happened. I stayed in the house as much as possible, telling my friends I was sick, but of course they still called. Like my best friend, Barb, who wanted to tell me about trips to the beach and the club. I couldn't tell her how I'd faced a Malignant One, or that I'd spoken with Alison Birkett. My parents asked me to keep it secret, but I would have anyway. I didn't want to push my luck.

I could talk to Paul, of course. And I did, except sometimes that just made it worse. Maybe I shouldn't say this, but he got so depressed, he kept saying how he was putting everybody in danger, how Lisa had 'corrupted' him and now it was too late, how we could back out if we wanted, how he wouldn't blame us and we should save ourselves—

One evening, Paul said to me, 'Maybe I'm making a mistake.'

At first I didn't want to answer. We were sitting in the living room – my folks had gone down to the den to watch TV – and I really just wanted to read. Finally I sighed and said, 'What kind of mistake?'

Paul sat with his elbows on his knees and a full cup of
coffee between his two hands. Great, I thought, just what
I needed, Paul spilling coffee on my mother's rug. 'I don't
know,' he said, 'Lisa kept saying she'd never hurt me.'

'She's a Malignant One,' I reminded him. 'It doesn't
matter what she says.'

'Yeah, I know. But sometimes you read about Malignant Ones helping people. Picking up some individual and,
you know, just doing things for him.'

'You mean like promotions?'

'Well, yeah. Lisa said she loved me, you know.' Before
I could say anything he rushed on, 'Sometimes you
see something on TV, about some great statesman, or
billionaire, who dies and they discover a Malignant One
helped him his whole life and that's how he became so rich
or important. And obviously the Malignant One didn't
harm him. It helped him. You know, Benign Ones won't
do that. They'll help you in some crisis, if they feel like
it, but they won't really take hold like that. Malignant
Ones—'

'First of all,' I said, 'you don't know what happens to
these great figures after they die.'

'Come on,' Paul said, 'you don't believe that old super-
stition about the dead suffering endless torture, do you?'

'That's not the point. You just don't know. And what
about all the stories of people who make deals with helpers
and suffer horrible agonies in *this* life? Like last month, on
20/20. Did you see that?'

He shook his head.

I said, 'Some woman in Arkansas summoned a Ferocious One to save her from bankruptcy. She ended up
in the hospital, vomiting crude oil for two weeks without
stopping. Do you want something like that to happen
to you?'

'No, of course not.'

'Paul. Listen to me. Malignant Ones are not good for
people. Okay? You got that?'

He smiled. 'Sure. Okay. It's just that she always said—'
'Paul?'

'All right. Okay.' He put down the coffee cup and came over to hug me. 'Thanks,' he said. 'You're the greatest kid cousin anyone ever had.'

'We're going to take care of you,' I said. 'Everything's going to be fine.'

For most of the thirteen days everything went pretty well. We had some small incidents. A couple of times when my folks or I answered the phone we heard a noise and then whoever (or whatever) it was hung up. Once, Paul picked up the phone and though he said nothing he started to sweat. My mother saw it first and shouted for my father who ran up and grabbed the receiver out of Paul's hand. After that, we forbade Paul to answer the phone. And several times people came to the door, with prizes they said, or government business (my father got a jury summons; he told the man to put it in the mailbox), even a box supposedly to make us part of the TV rating system. But nothing actually happened. And then, on a Sunday morning, my grandmother – or at least someone who looked and sounded just like her – showed up at the door.

'Mom!' my mother said. 'Um – hi.' Grandma never just shows up. And she never goes anywhere before three o'clock.

'Well?' Grandma said. 'Isn't anybody going to invite me in?'

I ran up before Mom could say anything. 'Make her say her name,' I said. Behind 'Grandma' I could see a car that looked just like hers. It even had the dent on the back fender and the Sacred Wildlife Fund sticker on the side window.

While Mom stood there looking confused and unhappy, Grandma said, 'Will somebody tell me what's going on? Why can't I just come in?' By now Daddy had joined us, and when I looked back I could see Paul standing in the kitchen doorway. 'Paul,' Grandma said, 'what are you doing here? Michael? Why is everyone acting so funny?'

'Say your name,' I told her. 'Say "My name is" and then your name.'

She laughed nervously. 'Ellen, what are you talking about?' To Mom, she said, 'Really, June, this is not very funny.'

Daddy ordered, 'Say it. Say "My name is" and then your name.'

Mom stared at the floor as her 'mother' said, 'June, I don't know what's going on with Ellen, but Mike too? And you? Are you going to take part in this silliness?'

Half crying, Mom said, very softly, 'It's part . . . part of a blessing enactment? You have to . . . For the house. Everyone has to say their name. Please.' She repeated, 'Please?'

'Well, I'm just sorry,' Grandma said. 'I thought I was welcome in my own daughter's house. Obviously, I was wrong.' She turned and headed for her car.

While my father closed the door, my mother stood crying, with her arms crossed over her chest in an X. 'I can't live like this,' she said. 'I just can't stand it.'

Daddy said, 'Honey, I'm sorry.' He reached out for her, but she twisted away. He added, 'You did that really well. I'm proud of you.'

'Don't patronize me!' she shouted at him. 'I don't want to do really well. I want a normal life.' She ran into the bathroom and slammed the door.

She was in there less than a minute when she started to shriek. Daddy and I came running, but the door was locked.' Honey,' Daddy shouted, 'open the door.' A sickening smell was washing over us and I suddenly realized my sneakers were getting wet. I looked down to see brown water coming under the door. Mom's screams died down as she fumbled open the lock. Inside, sewage was pouring out of the toilet – over the bowl, out the top of the tank, through cracks in the sides – 'Make it stop!'

Mom cried. Holding his hand over his face, Daddy sloshed through to the main valve. Looking back at me, he said, 'Ellen, get out of here. Run.' The handle came off in his hands. 'Shit,' he said.

I ran, but only to the basement where I shut off the main valve, and then back to the kitchen for the pump bottle. On the way, I could hear Paul, crying or something, but I couldn't pay any attention. When I got back to the bathroom my folks were stuffing things down the toilet bowl. Fighting not to vomit, I sprayed the toilet, the floor and the air, my parents, myself, all the while repeating the Standard Formula, as well as our own enactment spells and the ones the team had taught us. The flooding stopped. We all leaned against the walls, gasping.

'How am I going to clean this up?' Mom said. 'How can I clean this up?' I went into the living room and called Alison Birkett's office. When the answering service came on I told the woman 'My name is Ellen Pierson. I need to speak with Alison Birkett right away. It's an emergency.'

When the return call came I grabbed it before the first ring had even ended. 'This is Alison Birkett,' she said.

I took a breath and told her the story, trying to make it complete and concise. I'd been practising while I waited for her call.

Ms Birkett asked a few questions and then she said, 'My very deep apologies, Ms Pierson. I will send a clean-up team immediately. If it serves as any consolation, I suspect that this attack came as a last ditch effort by the enemy. Frustrated rage.'

'Last ditch?' I said.

'Do you think you and your family can come to my office tomorrow morning?'

'Yes,' I said, 'of course.'

'Good. It may not seem like it in the context, but I do have good news. 9 o'clock?'

'I'll tell my parents.'

'Fine. An escort will arrive at your house tomorrow at eight. Please be sure to convey my apologies to your parents and tell them that the clean-up team will be there within the hour.'

'I won't forget,' I said.

'I'm sure you won't,' Ms Birkett said. 'You've done very well, Ms Pierson. Very well indeed. I look forward to meeting you.'

'Thank you,' I managed to say. When we'd said goodbye and I'd hung up the phone I repeated to myself, ' "I look forward to meeting you". Wow.' Then I ran to tell my folks the news.

2

The office was a little smaller than I'd expected. There was a desk – some kind of dark red wood – and some leather-chairs, and walls of books, most of them in sets of twenty or so volumes. I wondered how many years you had to go to school to learn all that stuff.

Alison Birkett was a little fatter than she'd looked on the cover of *Time*. A little shorter, too, but otherwise she looked just like I'd imagined her as I lay awake half the night. Wavy red hair which she pushed back from her face. Narrow nose and wide mouth, which gave her face a lot of movement, a lot of expression. When she frowned, you really could see it. When she smiled, she let it take over her face. She wore a grey silk blouse open at the neck and with the sleeves rolled up slightly, and a straight dark purple skirt. Round her neck, on a silver chain, she wore the three peaked medallion of the Winged Lady of the Mountains. Just above her left wrist I could see a small crescent-shaped scar, a mark of initiation. She noticed my looking at it. Her eyes dropped to her arm and then back at me, and she smiled.

She shook all our hands and said our names without our telling her. When she came to me she nodded once and said, 'I'm very pleased to meet you, Ms Pierson.' Right there in front of my parents. If the chair hadn't been there I might have fallen over.

She sat down in a chair at the side of her desk, with her

legs out before her, crossed at the ankles. 'First of all,' she said, 'that disaster yesterday.'

'It was horrible,' my mother blurted. 'Absolutely horrible.'

Ms Birkett nodded. 'I know. Just hearing about it sickened me. I am very sorry you had to suffer such an outrage. As I told your daughter, however, it will not happen again. And the SDA will pay for the damage.'

'The SDA?' my father repeated.

'Let me explain what I've found out. To begin with, the F.I. request turned out to be quite a battle. Our government agencies do not like giving up their secrets. Especially the embarrassing ones.' She looked at Paul. He was breathing heavily. 'When we talked on the phone,' she said, 'you told me that your Lisa ran a temp agency.'

He said, 'That was her cover.'

'Oh no,' Ms Birkett said. 'That part of her story is actually true. Except that she does not find little typing jobs for secretaries. Lisa Black Dust – that's her proper designation, by the way – Lisa Black Dust 7 runs a temp agency for Malignant Ones.'

None of us spoke for a moment, then Mom said, 'I don't understand. You mean she hires out *demons*?'

Ms Birkett nodded. 'Precisely.'

Mom said, 'But who are their clients?'

Ms Birkett smiled again before she spoke. 'Corporations, lobbyists, large charitable organizations – but mostly the United States' government.'

My father whispered, 'Oh my God.' Paul moaned.

'The government?' I repeated.

'That's right. Various agencies, investigatory arms and, I suspect, the White House, though sections of the report came blacked out. "National Security Sanctification." One part that was not censored, however, described the involvement of one particular client of Black Dust 7. The Spiritual Development Agency hires her services on a very steady basis. When Mr Cabot and Ms Pierson came for help they spoke first to an underling. Someone "not in the loop" as the expression goes. When Mr Sebbick came on the case, however, the situation changed dramatically. For Mr Sebbick knew Lisa Black Dust 7's cover name and the location of her operation.'

I said, 'So the noble SDA tried to shut us up in order to protect themselves.'

'Exactly, Ms Pierson. And protect their convenient relationship. And they might have succeeded except for one factor their over-confidence failed to take into consideration. You and your family refused to let the matter drop. You contacted me.'

I grinned. 'Too bad for them they didn't get a Malignant Speaker to tell their fortunes.'

Ms Birkett laughed. 'Yes, and lucky for us.'

My father said, 'I'm glad you two find this so funny.'

'Not at all,' Ms Birkett said, but something of a smile remained. 'I assure you I recognize the urgency. In the past two weeks I have done little else but work on this case.'

Mom asked, 'But what do they do for the government?'

Ms Birkett shrugged. 'Spying, sabotage, manoeuvering decisions by other agencies, or even other governments. Possibly assassinations.'

'The French prime minister,' I blurted. 'His so-called heart attack.'

Her eyes narrowed, and then she nodded very slightly. 'I spoke out of turn,' she said. 'A bad habit. I think we had best keep such speculation amongst ourselves.'

I looked at the floor. 'Of course,' I said.

My mother said, 'This is horrible. It's . . . it's just horrible. How does the government pay the Malignant Ones?'

Ms Birkett said nothing for a moment, then, 'I don't think you want to know that.'

'Oh,' Mom said. 'Oh.'

Paul said, 'What am I going to do? What can I do?'

Ms Birkett said, 'You already have done it, Mr Cabot. *We* have done it.'

'I don't understand,' he said. But his voice sounded a little stronger.

Ms Birkett leaned back in her chair. 'We have something on them. We know something the government would not like to see published in the *New York Times*.'

Mom said, 'But what can we do with it? I mean, we can't just give interviews to the *Times*.'

'Please,' Ms Birkett said, 'I do not envision you appearing in the newspapers. Quite the contrary. The possibility is simply a threat, a weapon.'

'I still don't understand—' Mom said, but Ms Birkett stopped her. She held up a sheet of paper dense with writing and some sort of sacred seal stamped on the bottom. 'This,' she said, 'is a cease and desist order, issued this morning by Judge Malcom Bennett. Judge Bennett is a very useful man. A number of times, when the government and I have come to an agreement, Judge Bennett has given it the appearance of judicial compulsion.'

Daddy asked, 'What exactly do they cease and desist doing?'

'The order, in fact, does not restrain them so much as compel them. It requires the SDA to *cease* protecting Black Dust 7 and to *begin* protecting you and your family. In short, to do its duty.'

Mom said, 'But that horrible . . . that disgusting . . . yesterday—'

Ms Birkett nodded. 'The agreement came into effect at 12:01 this morning. Yesterday was Black Dust 7's last chance to express her rage. I had demanded immediate application, but the SDA argued that they needed time for their technicians to establish controls. Now they will pay for that mistake. I have already made some phone calls and begun the paperwork for damage claims.'

Daddy asked, 'Do you need information from us for the claims?'

'There's no hurry. Marjorie – my secretary – will get the details from you after the depossession process.'

'This court order,' Daddy said. 'It doesn't order them to stop hiring Malignant Ones to do its dirty work?'

She shook her head. 'No. It does require the government to cease all dealings specifically with Black Dust 7 and her agency. It does not, however, require anything further from them. The language is very careful.'

'And we don't go to the *Times*?'

'No. What purpose would it serve? This agreement secures your safety. If we expose the government, that will remove the incentive to protect you. We certainly don't want any repeats of what happened yesterday. Or worse. And I assure you, the government will continue to deal with Malignant Ones, no matter how much we expose this particular arrangement.'

I said, 'So we just let them continue.' As soon as I'd said it, I wished I could take it back. I felt so ungrateful.

Ms Birkett said, 'I'm afraid so, Ms Pierson. We take the victory we can get.'

'I'm sorry,' I said. 'I mean, thank you.'

Paul asked, 'How can we trust the SDA? They could say they're protecting me – us – and do nothing.'

Ms Birkett said, 'Of course. That is why I have demanded that my own team monitor the entire depossession process. And remember, the threat of exposure will remain.'

My father asked, 'What's to stop them just – getting rid of all of us? If we're gone, we can't expose them.'

'They would have to get rid of me as well. And I have created various information-dumping routines "in the event of my untimely disappearance" as they say in the movies.'

'Wow,' I said.

Paul said, 'What about afterwards? How do I know she'll leave me alone?'

'Because of the protection the SDA will give you. And because it will suit the government for you to remain unharmed. And the government will make sure it suits the Malignant Ones.'

Daddy asked, 'But can the Malignant Ones themselves control her?'

'Oh yes. The Bright Beings, the Benign Ones and the Malignant Ones together, actually form something of a single entity. The individual Beings appear to us as separate, like people, but we might describe them better as branches of that one entity. Configurations, to use the proper term.' She paused. 'The point is, they can control her, and they will.'

Paul said, 'What about my job? Am I going to have to walk past the damn temp agency every time I go to work?'

'Certainly not,' Ms Birkett said. 'All traces of Lisa Black Dust 7 and her agency will vanish from the building.' She smiled. 'When you return to work, your colleagues will no doubt tell you of the week the government shut down the building. "Resanctification of an architectural landmark" I believe they will call it.'

We stayed in her office a little bit longer, talking about what would happen, what the SDA would do, how they would reseal our house and purify Paul's apartment, how they would take us to a depossession centre, how we'd have to sit around in quarantine for a week but nothing would hurt.

Finally we had to leave. My folks shook her hand and hurried out of the office. Paul shook her hand, too, but he didn't look at her. I think he was crying.

The escort team, two women without any masks but carrying government sanctified electronic spirit dispersers, waited in the doorway. They looked bored. I got up last and shook her hand, trying to do it as strong as she did. I was halfway to the door when she called to me. 'Ellen,' she said, and I turned. She was smiling. 'I've enjoyed meeting you,' she said. 'If you find yourself downtown, please feel free to drop in on me.'

'Oh yes,' I said. 'Yes, I will. Thank you. Thank you very much.' And then I left.

The depossession took five days. To be honest, it was mostly kind of dull. We had to go to an SDA safe house upstate, along the Hudson. It was very pretty, with views of the cliffs and lots of woods. Except we didn't get to look around much. We chanted and sweated and wrote things on paper and made 'substitutes' (dolls, that is; you should have seen my father's!). At least we got to do some stuff down by the river, at night. Most of the time, however, I had to sit in my room, or else lie down on a surgical table while people in lab coats and sanctified masks (I kept looking for the crocodile woman but she never showed) smeared creams and smelly oils on me and wiped them off, or painted pictures and wrote words on my belly, or else ran tests with electrodes attached to my head, lights shining in my face, and so on.

I don't know what I was expecting, maybe the building shaking, slime pouring out of the walls, shrieks and wild laughter – you know, the kind of thing you see on TV shows.

Only once did something really weird happen, and it wasn't the kind of thing you expect. It was night time and they'd taken me down to the river again, a small cove with a ring of metal poles near the edge of the water. My caseworker tied a black silk blindfold around my eyes and then directed me to sit down in the centre of the ring. The poles gave off a low rhythmic hum.

For a while I just thought about school or something. Slowly, the hum got louder and my head started to hurt. Suddenly, I heard giggles behind me. I turned my head, frightened. Why were the techs giggling? But the sound came from somewhere further back, somewhere in the woods.

I reached up to pull off the blindfold. 'No,' my caseworker said. 'Leave it on.' My hand didn't move, just held on to the cloth. 'Leave it alone,' the caseworker said. I let go.

The giggling got louder, then changed to moans and sighs. I could hear voices, though I couldn't hear what they said. Until a voice I knew said, 'Two is lovely, but three's a feast. Ellen?' I pulled off the blindfold. Outside the circle of poles, beyond the stupid techs who didn't seem to notice anything at all, Lisa Black Dust 7 and Alison Birkett lay naked together at the edge of the trees.

'No!' I shouted, or something dumb like that, and covered my eyes with my hands.

'Don't leave the circle,' my caseworker told me. I could hardly hear her, the roaring in the poles had gotten so loud. It ran from pole to pole, round and round the ring. 'What do you see?' the caseworker asked. I shook my head. Alison Birkett's voice called my name again.

When I looked again, she and Black Dust 7 were kissing each other and doing things with their hands I don't want to describe. And suddenly I could feel them touching me, sliding invisible hands all over my body. I thrashed around like someone slapping away a swarm of bugs.

'Don't leave,' my caseworker said again, but I just shouted at her, 'Shut up!' Okay, I told myself, don't panic. Trying to ignore the laughter and those horrible hands all over me, I closed my eyes, took a breath – and said all the formulas and prayers the techs had been teaching me over the past few days. The laughter died away, the hands became feathers.

And I wanted them back. I wanted to stop the chants and the formulas, I wanted to bring back the voices, the hands. I felt so lonely, so ashamed. Alison Birkett would hate me, no one would ever love me. No one ever *had* loved me. But now these two wonderful beings had come to rescue mc. Why was I driving them away? Didn't I know they only played a game, pretending to be enemies so they could trick the idiots, like my parents and the SDA? They couldn't fool me, they knew that. I was much too smart for any of that. Why was I driving them away? If I joined them the three of us could do anything. They needed me, Alison Birkett needed me. If I turned her down now, she'd never speak to me again.

Thank mine and everyone else's guardians that the caseworker didn't say or do anything. I'm sure if I'd heard that whining voice I would have given up the protections just to spite her. Instead, I clenched my fists and said as loud as I could, 'Ferocious One, I beg you to release me. I know that nothing I have done deserves your Malignant Intervention.' I repeated it twice more, louder each time. Inner conviction, they say, is half the working. When I opened my eyes again, they were gone.

I wondered a lot what Paul was going through. If the monster could do that to me, what would happen to my poor cousin, the only one of us who'd actually given in to her? I only saw him once during our time in the safe house. I saw him at the other end of a corridor. I called to him but he turned away, and then my own caseworker pushed me into another lab room.

After five days they pronounced us 'free and liberated'. Just like the Pentagon, I thought. We shouldn't have any more trouble they assured us. But just in case, they gave us each a silver medallion to wear around our necks, charged and sanctified in the SDA laboratories and triggered with our own special enactment prayer. We had to say the prayer when we woke up or went to sleep or ate anything ('even a piece of chewing gum' my caseworker told me) or washed our hands or went to the bathroom – but especially if we felt afraid. 'Remember,' my caseworker said, 'fear is the danger sign. Don't ignore it. Don't convince yourself it's nothing or it's just nervousness. In all likelihood it will be nothing, but don't ignore it. Any time you feel afraid, say your protection.'

We were standing on the lawn and she was giving me a last-minute lecture, but I was really just looking for Paul. I knew my folks had finished, but where was Paul? Suddenly I saw him, in the doorway shaking hands with his own caseworker. He was laughing.

'Paul!' I shouted, and ran over and hugged him. I felt like a dumb kid, but I couldn't help myself. He looked so wonderful, so healthy. He separated from me, grinned, then hugged me again. He was wearing a shirt I'd never seen before. It looked new and I wondered if his caseworker had given it to him.

Ms Birkett's people drove us home. I wanted to ask how they liked working for her and stuff like that, but it didn't feel like the time. My folks said almost nothing, just stared out the window. Paul did most of the talking. He talked about getting back to work, about whether he should give back the promotions (he laughed when he said it, and then added 'But why shouldn't I get something out of this? I've sure as hell suffered enough.'), how great it was not to feel scared all the time, how he almost wished he could have seen Lisa's face when they banished her from the building. And yet, when he stopped talking and turned to the window, I could see him trembling.

I didn't see Paul too much during the next few weeks. We talked a couple of times, and he told me a little about all the questions they'd asked him about Lisa and what he'd done with her. But nothing about what had happened to him over the five days in the safe house. And then he stopped calling me, and to be honest I didn't call him.

I didn't see Alison Birkett, either. I don't know why, I kept wanting to call her, to make up some excuse why I had to go downtown so I could visit her. But somehow I never did it. It wasn't because of what had happened by the river. At least I don't think it was. I mean, I knew very well that the thing with Black Dust 7 was not Alison

Birkett. But maybe I thought if I saw her I would have to tell her. I don't know. So instead, I went to the library and read about her, everything I could find.

I also didn't see much of my friends. The thing was, I still couldn't tell them. The agreement with the government demanded that we keep the whole thing secret. I guess I could have made up some story how I'd met Alison Birkett, but what was the point if I couldn't give the real reason? And I didn't feel much like talking with them if I couldn't talk about everything that had happened. So I mostly went to the library, or stayed home and watched TV, or else rode my bike down to the shore.

And every day I said my words. And did my enactments and made my offerings.

Three weeks passed before the 'incident' happened. That's what the newspapers called it later. There were two, really, mine and Paul's, but Paul's was more spectacular. My incident took place in a teashop on Northern Boulevard, near my home. I'd been down in the library, feeling sleepy, so I thought, I know, I'll go have some tea. Ye Village Tea Parlore (no kidding, that's really what they called it) had just opened, selling lots of herb teas and gooey cakes and yoghurt and blueberry scones.

So I was sitting there at a glass-topped iron table in a pink chair that hurt my back, when this kid came in. He looked about my age, but he sure didn't look like anyone from this neighbourhood. He wore a torn T-shirt and dumpy jeans and shoes with big holes in them. And he started to spray paint graffiti all over the walls. I couldn't believe it. Just coming in off the street like that. I turned around, figuring someone would come charging from the kitchen to throw him out. Instead, the waitress and the owner just stood there, watching. And then they turned to me. And smiled. With my face. They looked just like me, except they were versions of me all pitted with disease.

I looked again at the graffiti. My name was all over it. And the rest of it – it went on and on about blood and filth and lot of things I don't want to repeat. Behind me one of the women laughed, an hysterical giggle.

Don't panic, I ordered myself. *You're protected*. I grabbed hold of my medallion. It felt hot in my hand – like it was angry. I whispered my private formula. The boy's grin faded. Behind me the laughter stopped. I said the protection again, louder this time. The boy's face spasmed and he dropped his spray can. Wow. I grinned. You bastards, I thought, I've got something that can make you hurt.

I was tempted to go after them, but instead I just got myself out of there. I backed out of the door, and when I got to my bike I held on tight to my medallion and kept saying the words while I fumbled open the lock. Finally I got it free and rode off as fast as I could.

When I got home I dropped the bike on the lawn and ran up to my room where I called Alison Birkett. 'Damn,' she said (in the middle of everything I really liked an adult cursing and not apologizing). 'This should not have happened. This is not going to happen again.'

'Can I come see you?' I asked.

'Yes,' she said. 'Yes, please do. And I'll start making some phone calls. I apologize to you, Ms Pierson. This should not have happened.'

I called my mother and told her I'd be back a little later than I'd thought, then rode my bike to the train station. When I got to the office, Ms Birkett had just heard from Paul. He'd been in a taxi which had started going faster and faster, until he realized the driver planned to drive it straight into the side of Paul's office building. At the last moment, Paul said his protection and the taxi suddenly blew out all four tyres so that it grated to a stop halfway up the sidewalk. In the middle of all the screaming people Paul escaped the car and ran up to his office, where he locked the door and called Ms Birkett.

While she told me the news, she kept her fist clenched. I kept expecting her to bang it on the desktop. She also told me how Paul had encountered signs all week long and ignored them. The phone would ring and he'd hear nothing but liquid sounds, like running water. Once, he was taking a shower and the water became incredibly sweet, like perfume. And one night he was watching TV when instead of a commercial he just heard a soft voice calling his name over and over.

'That's one way they work,' Ms Birkett said. 'They lure you off your guard with subtle seduction, and then they attack. Your cousin should have called me immediately. I suspect his laxness emboldened them to attack you as well. But' – and she pointed a finger at the air – 'that does not excuse this happening. The government assured us that the Beings would control Black Dust 7. If anything, it sounds like they're helping her.' She picked up the phone. 'Marjorie,' she said, 'get me Jack Moralty on the phone. Right now.'

Wow, I thought. The head of the SDA. 'Do you want me to wait outside?' I said.

'No,' she said, and switched on the speaker. 'I want you to hear this.' For eight minutes (I timed it) she shouted at Jonathan Moralty. She was sarcastic, she threatened him, she sounded like a school principal putting down a gym teacher. At the end, he swore to her that it would not happen again, that the defence would hold, that he could and would compel 'the other side' to keep their commitments and constrain Black Dust 7. He promised to investigate, to let her know ('in days, not weeks' she told him) who had let down their guard, what had happened, what he was going to do about it, and on and on. It was incredible. 'Wow,' I said as she hung up the phone. I grinned at her. 'Wow.'

She smiled back at me, not really like an adult to a child, more like another kid. 'Sometimes,' she said, 'you have to talk tough to these people.' There was a pause and then we both started to laugh. 'Oh God,' she said, still laughing. 'I sound like a gangster movie.' That set us off all over again.

After that, I felt kind of embarrassed. 'I guess I better go,' I said.

She ignored me. 'Tell me about yourself,' she said. So I told her about where I live, and school, and how a lot of times the other kids all seemed like jerks to me. She nodded and said she used to feel that way too. 'Still do, sometimes,' she said, and we both laughed again. Then she asked me if I knew what I wanted to study in college. I didn't dare look at her as I said, 'I kind of thought I would study demonic law.'

She didn't say anything personal or cute. She just said, 'It's a good profession. A lot of work, a long time to study. But it can be worth it. When you apply to colleges, let me know. I'll write a recommendation.'

My mouth fell open. It really did, just like they say in stories. 'Thank you,' I said finally. 'Thank you very much.' I could just imagine those college admission officers opening up yet another application envelope and finding a rec letter from Alison Birkett.

I went home a little after that. I didn't look forward to facing my parents. I thought they would ground me or something for running off to Ms Birkett by myself, but all they cared about was the attack. How could it happen, they wanted to know. Didn't Alison Birkett say Lisa Black Dust 7 was just a branch of a single entity? What did it mean? Though it kind of excited me that they were questioning *me*, I finally got them to call Ms Birkett. After half an hour shouting on the phone they calmed down. A few days later, the official SDA report came. It didn't say that much really, just promised extra vigilance, greater surveillance, that sort of thing. After a few weeks without any trouble, things sort of got back to normal.

Over the next couple of months I came into town to visit Ms Birkett about once a week. They weren't very

long visits. I'd go in with my father, or Mom if she needed
to go shopping, and I'd stop by the office for maybe half
an hour, then meet Mom or take the train home. A couple
of times she took me to lunch. When school started it was
a little harder, but Ms Birkett often worked Saturdays and
my folks sometimes went into town for cultural stuff on
Saturday so that worked out.

Maybe I should have spent some of that time with Paul.
Maybe if I'd been there for him things wouldn't have
happened the way they did. I did go see him pretty soon
after the incidents. I was excited, actually, and I guess I
went on too much about the stuff Ms Birkett had said
on the phone and how she'd treated the SDA head like
a bad boy. Paul didn't seem to care. He tried to smile a
few times, but mostly he just sat bent over, not saying
anything.

I think I got annoyed with him, because I started to
attack him for not reporting the strange phone calls and
the other stuff that had happened.

'But they weren't anything bad,' he said.

'Not bad?' I yelled. 'That cab driver almost drove you
into a building.'

'I mean the things before that,' he said. 'Some of them
were kind of nice. Like the smell in the shower.'

'Ms Birkett says that's how they pull you in. Get you
to lower your guard.'

Paul shrugged. 'I guess.'

'Paul,' I said, 'I want you to promise me you'll protect
yourself. Please.'

He smiled at me. 'Sure.'

'Promise you'll report any strange events. Even pleas-
ant ones.'

Still smiling, he nodded. 'Okay. I promise.' We hugged
each other, but when I let him go, he just sat there
again.

'It's just . . . I don't know. Sometimes I just feel so
lonely.'

'You can always call me,' I said.

'You know,' Paul said, 'she always said she would never harm me.'

'Paul!' I yelled at him.

He held up a hand. 'I know, I know,' he said. 'I promise.'

'And promise you'll call me if you feel lonely.'

'Okay,' he said. 'It's a deal.'

I know I should never have taken his word. I know I should have kept after him. Maybe made him see a therapist or something, someone to wave rattles over his head and 'travel the circles of his inner being' (I read that once in a brochure). But instead, I just went off on my own. With Alison.

But I was with him when it happened. I saw it even though I couldn't stop it. In a horrible kind of way I'm glad about that. I would have hated it if Alison Birkett had told me on the telephone.

What happened was that I went to see Paul one day. I'd like to say I was worried about him, but what really happened was that my folks had been complaining about my seeing Ms Birkett too much. My mother even said it was 'sick', until I screamed at her to take it back. So when I had a day off from school I called Paul and got him to invite me for lunch. It was the only way I could get into the city. I figured that after lunch he would go back to work and I could stop in at the office.

He seemed really happy to see me. We went to a Chinese restaurant where everybody stared at us for laughing so hard. I loved seeing him like that. But then, when he paid the bill and we started back, his mood collapsed. He stopped joking, he mumbled or said nothing when I spoke to him.

By the time we reached his building I was starting to get angry. Why was I wasting time with this mopey slouch cousin of mine? I almost walked away from him at the bronze and glass door leading into the lobby. But I followed him in, along with a couple of men and women in suits.

Paul's building was one of those early model office towers, with overlapping plates of steel outside and lots of polished wood and brass inside. A mosaic of the Army of the Saints driving the Malignant Ones out of New Chicago filled the floor of the circular lobby. Usually the building super kept the floor all clean and shiny. It's a big tourist attraction and helps keep the rent high. That day, the tiles looked all dull, as if someone had tracked mud and gas station grease all over them. When I looked at it I felt queasy, but Paul didn't seem to notice, even though he walked with his head down.

We went to the row of elevators, with their glossy walnut doors. In a moment, I thought, I can get rid of him. Go see Alison.

I started to hear voices. Crowds of whispers, hisses, laughter, people shouting something too far away for me to make out what they were saying. I looked around, surprised. There were only about twenty people in the whole lobby. It's in my head, I realized. *Get out of my head*. I stamped on the floor, hit my hands against the side of my head. And then the elevator door opened.

A bright light burst out of the steel box. I shouted and jumped back. When I could see again the elevator floor heaved and rolled. I shook my head and stared. The floor was covered with snakes.

I started to scream. People were screaming all around me, climbing all over each other to get away. I started to run. But Paul just stood there. He looked at the snakes with his mouth hanging open, like a baby watching TV. 'Paul!' I shouted. 'Run. Get away from there.' He turned towards me and squinted, as if the light in the elevator had blinded him. A second later he was back looking at the snakes.

I've seen snakes at the zoo and usually they don't make any noise. But these were deafening, more of a buzz than a hiss, and it got louder and louder every second, making me feel like my head would crack open. When I said my formula of protection I stumbled over the words twice before I could get it right.

Holding on to my medallion with one hand I grabbed Paul's arm. 'Get away from there!' I screamed at him. 'Say your formula. Say it!' He shoved me and I fell back on the floor. As loud as I could I said my own formula and then the Standard Recognition. In my head the buzzing softened. But in the elevator the snakes didn't go away. Paul covered his ears. 'Paul!' I called again. He turned to me and shrugged. When he stepped into the elevator the door closed behind him.

I ran up and kicked the doors, hit them as hard as I could. 'Give him back!' I yelled. 'You promised! Give him back.' Someone grabbed me. A cop, I think. A moment later a needle slid into my arm. I remember I looked at it amazed and then tried to pull my arm away. Too late. 'Ferocious One,' I said. 'Please release me . . .' And then the drug hit me and I was gone.

I woke up in a hospital bed with my mother slumped over in a chair next to me. 'Mom?' I said, and her head jerked up.

'Ellen,' she said. 'Thank God.'

For some reason my arms were folded across my body. I tried to reach out a hand but couldn't. Shit, I thought, I'm paralyzed. But when I flexed my muscles there was nothing wrong with them. The hospital, or the cops, had tied me into a restraining sheet. I tilted up my head to look at it. Sky blue, with an eye of power in the centre radiating circles of protection, it held me like a huge bandage, with my arms pulled over each other like someone about to bow in a sacred pose of purification. 'Get this off me,' I said.

'Honey, please,' Mom said.

'Get this goddamn thing off me.'

My mother stuck her head out the door. 'Help,' she

called, and just like in the movies a couple of nurses came running into my room.

Looking up at their masked faces (a duck and a pig) I tried to sound as calm as possible. 'Do you mind telling me what this is about?' I said, nodding my head at the sheet.

'For your own protection,' the duck grunted. She should be wearing the pig mask, I thought.

'Well, can you take it off me?' I said.

The duck said to her pal, 'Go get the portscan, okay?' So I had to wait while they wheeled in a white machine with lots of dials and screens, and long wires with tiny rubber tips at the end to place against my face, head, heart and groin.

'How do I configure?' I asked the pig.

Instead of answering she said to the other nurse, 'Readings all fall within the 210–225 range.'

I asked, 'Is that normal?' She hesitated, then nodded. 'Great,' I said, 'now will you unstrap me?' They didn't move. I looked at my mother. 'Mom,' I said, 'can you get them to take this off me?'

'Honey,' she said, and stopped. Her face scrunched up.

I realized suddenly why they didn't want to unstrap me. 'Oh God,' I said. 'Paul.' I could still see his shrug before he stepped into the elevator. 'Where is he?' I asked. Nobody answered. 'He's dead, isn't he? They got him. Tell me they got him.'

My mother just nodded. When I started to cry she came and reached toward my face with a crumpled tissue, but I did my best to turn my head. I guess crying was the right response, because a few moments later the nurses undid the sheet and I could blow my own nose.

The hospital kept me overnight. Observation. I didn't mind. I didn't want to think. I don't think I wanted to go home. Some time in the afternoon I suddenly noticed stitches on my right arm just below the elbow. It didn't look like a wound. It was too neat. It looked more like surgery. 'What's this?' I asked my mother.

Once again, she looked all embarrassed, even ashamed. Finally, she said, 'It's a chip.'

'A chip? What do you mean?'

'A microchip,' she said. She held out her arm and pushed up the sleeve of her blouse. 'Look,' she said, 'I've got one too. The hospital put them in. Daddy too.'

'Why are they sticking microchips in us?'

'It's . . . it's to monitor what happens.' She looked so scared she could hardly talk. 'They said this way they could intervene if . . . if anyone . . . anything should threaten us. They'll know before it happens, they said.'

'Great,' was all I could say. 'Terrific.' Goddamn them, I thought. Why couldn't they have given one to Paul? Stupid bastards.

With the chip in, the hospital let me walk around. After visiting hours that night, when my folks had gone, I just went up and down the floor. I thought of watching TV or calling people on the pay phone at the nurses' station. But I just kept walking until they gave me a pill and sent me to bed. I remember some Ragged Healer by the side of my bed, hopping from one bare foot to the other, and shaking maracas over me as I was falling asleep.

There was one phone call especially I thought of making. My folks had told me that Alison Birkett had wanted to come see me, but thought she should ask first. Good thing, I told them. Because I didn't want to see her. I had her home phone number, though, and after my folks left I kept thinking of calling her. Except I didn't.

At home the next few days, I didn't do much more than I'd done in the hospital. My folks didn't push me to go back to school. Most of the time I sat in my room. I tried to read or watch TV, but couldn't concentrate. When the phone rang, I just let it go on and on and didn't answer.

And then, on the fourth day I was home, I put on the all-news cable station. And there lay my cousin Paul, all alone in an empty elevator, his hands and face so puffed up you could hardly tell he was a human being and not some lump of clay stuffed into a suit.

I didn't cry or scream. I just sat there, watching the TV and shaking. When the report ended – I didn't hear a word – I grabbed the framed picture of Alison Birkett – it still hung above my desk – and threw it at the TV as hard as I could. Then I grabbed all the money I could find and jumped on my bike to head for the train station.

When I got to the office it was almost like Marjorie, her secretary, had been waiting for me. She jumped up from her desk to tell me, 'You can't go in there.'

'Get out of my way,' I ordered.

'She's in conference,' Marjorie insisted.

'With whom? Jack Moralty? The president? God?' When I tried to run around her she grabbed my arm.

I heard a voice I'd once thought was the most beautiful sound I knew. 'For heaven's sake,' Alison Birkett said, 'let her in.' Marjorie dropped my arm and I stood there, out of breath, just looking at her.

She looked all worn out, like somebody in pain, or someone who's been crying for days. It shocked me, but it didn't make me feel better. Over her shoulder she said, 'Robert, will you please excuse me? I'm sorry to break off our talk. I'll have to get back to you later.' Someone mumbled something and then a man in a suit left the office. 'Come in,' Ms Birkett said. 'Please.'

Inside her office, she knew better than to offer me a seat. We just stood there, looking at each other. Finally, Ms Birkett said, 'I'm sorry, Ellen. I'm so, so sorry.'

'Why?' I said. 'Because your little scheme failed? Because you've tarnished your perfect reputation?'

She just said again, 'I'm sorry, Ellen. Please believe me.'

'I believed you when you said you'd protect him. I fell for all your big buddy buddy talk with the goddamn SDA. I believed you!'

'And I believed it would work.'

'Why? Why didn't you realize? You're the expert. You're supposed to know everything, do everything.'

Her face looked like it would break apart and I thought, *don't you dare, don't you dare cry*. She said, 'I thought . . . I thought the SDA could control them. And I thought I controlled the SDA. Oh God, I was so stupid.'

'I trusted you,' I said.

'I know. And Paul trusted me. That poor boy. Ellen . . . I . . . I'm—' She stopped. I guess she realized she'd already said how sorry she was.

I said, 'He just wanted love. That's all he wanted.'

'Love and power,' Alison Birkett said. 'Just like all of us.'

And that did it. I don't know why, but I just started to cry. I wanted to leave, but I couldn't, all I could do was run on like a double faucet, with my shoulders jerking up and down. She held open her arms, timidly, halfway. I might have resisted if she'd been more confident. Instead, I half stepped, half fell into her hug.

I don't know how long she held me. It felt like a long time. I think she was crying with me, but I'm not sure, I was crying enough for both of us. When I stopped and pulled loose from her, I didn't know what to do, if I should say something, or run out of the office.

Alison said, 'I understand the SDA put a chip in you.'

I shrugged. 'Yeah. I guess they told you.'

'I might as well let you know,' she said. 'I got them to tell me the frequencies and I've had my own teams monitoring the readings day and night. We can no longer trust the SDA for anything.' When I didn't answer, we both just stood there.

That's when she brought up the other thing, the part of this I'd known would come up sooner or later. 'Ellen,' she said, 'there's something we need to talk about. I don't know if this is the right time, but I'm not sure there'll ever be a right time.' She waited. When I didn't answer, she sighed, 'I suppose you know what I'm going to ask. I'm sure you've thought about it. I'll have to speak to your parents as well, but I wanted to ask you first. The question is this: do we fight? Do we go public?'

Well, I had thought about it. I'd imagined her asking me that question, or something like it, and I believed I wouldn't know what to say. I thought I didn't care. But I didn't even hesitate, I answered right away. 'Yes,' I said, and my hands amazed me by clenching into fists. 'I want to get them. I want to make them hurt.'

She sighed. 'You're too smart not to know what will happen. Especially after that damn TV spectacle of Paul in the elevator. The reporters will be all over you. You, your parents, anyone they can find. The magazines, the newspapers and especially the TV people, they'll come at you like an army of Malignant Ones themselves.'

'And you,' I said.

She shrugged. 'It's my job. With me, they'll come to my office. With you, they'll come to your house.'

I said, 'Maybe *Nightline* will hire Lisa Black Dust 7.'

She smiled. 'Maybe they already have.'

'I want to fight.'

'Yes, I know. I do too. You have no idea how much I want that. I want to go after them more than I've wanted anything in a very long time. But please, Ellen, think about it. At least until I speak with your parents. I . . . I can try to protect you. I'm certainly not going to promise. Not after what's happened. But if we do fight I will do everything I can to help all of you. With the media as well as the enemy. And I do promise never to take you or your safety for granted.'

Well, it turned out that just getting my folks to talk with Ms Birkett took a couple of weeks. She'd tried to call them, apparently, and my father had threatened her, while my mother had simply refused to speak at all. When I tried to push them into a discussion of what we should do they pulled the 'you're just a kid' routine on me.

I figured Daddy was the weak link and went to work on him. I played up all his anger at government cover-ups, at corruption, at the SDA having too much power. But he was scared. It was one thing to shout and shake his fist, but another to actually do anything. When I tried to talk about Paul, and not just the government, he always changed the subject.

It really amazed me when my mother turned out to be the one to give in. I hadn't even really talked with her about it, though a couple of times she'd intervened between me and my father. But I knew how scared she was. I saw her once doing the laundry. She opened the washing machine lid and jumped back, as if snakes would come slithering out at any moment. And a couple of times I'd caught her gripping her amulet really hard, with her eyes closed and her lips moving. And then one night we were all sitting at dinner, none of us saying anything, and Mom looked like she wanted to cry, and I was thinking, great, just what I need, when suddenly she banged her fist on the table, and said, 'Damn! Damn, damn, damn.'

Daddy stared down at his plate a moment, then he got up to walk over to her. 'Honey,' he said, and tried to put his arms around her.

She pushed him away. She *growled* and pushed him away. I'd never heard her growl before. She looked up at him, and even though her head was shaking no, she said, 'I want to go see Alison Birkett.'

So we did it. It took several more days of discussion – especially about the precautions we needed to take, the extra teams Ms Birkett had brought in to watch over us (she had them implant a second chip in each of us, with frequencies known only to her staff), the methods to make sure the story got out if anything happened to us – but we finally did it. We all sat there in the office, Daddy and Mommy and I all holding hands, while Alison called the *New York Times* and offered them the biggest story since the Pentagon scandal.

Maybc you saw the headlines. 'Man Found Dead In Elevator Was Under SDA Protection.' That's how we started. Alison said we should break the story 'in increments' to let it build. But it didn't take long for the blockbuster to get out. If I'd wanted, I could have saved another *Time* cover. And *Newsweek* too. I still remember the *Newsweek* one. That repulsive picture of Paul's body and above it, in flaming letters, 'Demonic Corruption', with smaller letters underneath: 'Alison Birkett Accuses US Government Of Hiring And Protecting Malignant Ones.'

That was half the attack, the media pressure. The other half was a lawsuit against the SDA. We charged them with malfeasance, malpractice and various other mals, and demanded $10,000,000 in damages. At first the idea overwhelmed me. Alison Birkett and I were suing the SDA! But somehow, I don't know, after a while it kind of sickened me. That we might get rich because Paul fell for some stupid Ferocious One. Paul had hoped to get rich. All that talk about promotions. And now the snakes had gotten him, and we were asking for $10,000,000.

In a way, we did need money, if not that much. Alison had her teams watching over me and my folks day and night. As well as checking our personal readings, they monitored the house, Daddy's office, even my school. At the moment, she was paying them herself, but she couldn't keep that up for long. And of course, when you ask for a lot of money you get more publicity than if you ask for a little. Even so, I didn't like it.

I felt kind of rotten about the media uproar too. At first, it knocked me out, the idea of being on television. But then it just exhausted and finally disgusted me. Actually, Alison did a pretty good job of shielding me. She managed to break the news in ways that emphasized the government's part in what happened and not me and my folks (she even apologized to me for 'trivializing' my 'heroism'). Maybe you saw that creep John Sebbick squirming on *60 Minutes*. I enjoyed that one.

Still, just being Paul's closest relatives guaranteed us all a place on, you guessed it, *Nightline*, and anyone else who could get a hold of us. At least after a couple of weeks the interest in us faded, revived only a little by the lawsuit. (I still remember a letter that described Mom and Dad as 'tawdry money-grubbers trying to cash in on a genuine tragedy.' How can people write such things about someone they don't even know?)

I did have to stay home from school for a while. I even had to stay off the street. People would recognize me from TV and think that that entitled them to come up and talk to me. Usually, they gave me the 'poor dear child' routine, but a couple of people ran away or made hand signs of protection against me. One woman started screaming at me. Apparently she thought I had summoned the Malignant Ones to attack Paul and now would do the same thing to her. That same day, a woman in the supermarket recognized my mother and actually pronounced the Standard Formula against her.

But even that kind of craziness died down and we went back more or less to our normal lives. I was a big deal in school for a while. I noticed that a lot of the kids, and the teachers too, couldn't seem to decide whether they wanted to hang around with me or get as far away from me as possible. Some parents tried to ban me from the school as a danger to their own kids. Nothing personal, they assured everyone, but what would happen if Lisa Black Dust 7 sent her snakes at me in the school cafeteria? But when everything stayed safe over a couple of months, and I stopped showing up on their evening news, everyone lost interest. I could go back to being a kid again.

The lawsuit just seemed to get stuck in technicalities. Ms Birkett assured me it was moving along, but it looked to me more like a legal video game between her and the government. Outside the suit, the scandal bogged down in debates about special prosecutors versus congressional hearings. A lot of lawyers and constitutional experts worked themselves into a frenzy arguing about whether the Bill of Rights covered 'non-human entities' and whether Ms Birkett, or Congress, could legally compel Bright Beings to testify. That's where it looked like things would stay for a long time.

And then I started seeing Paul.

The first time was on a billboard near my school. It was lunchtime and I'd gone for a walk after eating by myself. I'd been doing a lot of stuff by myself. It wasn't that people were shunning me. They'd mostly gotten over that. I just felt, I don't know, kind of strange around my friends. Anyway, after lunch I went for a walk to a candy store. I had to pass this cutesy billboard which shows a guy in a sports car waving his hand. They've got it rigged so the metal hand actually moves back and forth. Now, I've seen this thing hundreds of times. I never look at it any more. But that day I looked up as I came towards it – and the man in the car was Paul.

He didn't look like Paul, he was Paul. The waving hand even wore Paul's initiation ring from college. 'Paul!' I shouted.

A car jerked to a stop. A man about sixty leaned his head out. 'I'm sorry,' he said, 'I don't think I know you.'

I stared at him. 'Huh?' I said, or something equally clear.

He sighed. 'You called me. I'm Paul, right?'

'No,' I said. 'I mean, I didn't mean you. I meant him.' I pointed up at the billboard. The man next to me shook his head, muttered something and drove off. I just stood there, squinting up at the billboard. Because when I'd looked again, the face had returned to its normal bland nothing, with the hand empty of rings or marks of any kind.

I went back to school and somehow got through the afternoon. On the way home, I wondered if I should tell my folks, or Ms Birkett. I don't think I made an actual decision not to tell them. I just didn't.

Just as I didn't think about it. Or tried not to. For a week, whenever it came into my mind, I did my best to push it away. Somewhere in my head, I was wondering why the monitor teams hadn't picked up anything and if their precautions would turn out as useless with me as they did with Paul. Then one night I was lying in bed, watching the little television my folks had given me to replace the one I smashed throwing Alison's picture at it. I should have been sleeping, with school the next day, but I felt so awake. So I watched some soap about a bunch of pilgrims on their way to the Beach of Marvels in Northern California, and then the news. And then came one of those talk shows where everybody's lively and no one's ever depressed or suffering. And you know how they always start with the announcer blaring the name of the host and the audience goes wild? Well, this time the announcer shouted out the usual stuff about live from Hollywood and all the wonderful guests, and then suddenly he said, 'And here comes . . . Paul!' And sure enough, there came my cousin, dancing out from behind the curtains, waving his hands, bowing and grinning in mock embarrassment at the adulation of his fans.

Well, I screamed. I screamed so loud I don't know how the windows stayed in the walls. Seconds later, my folks came tumbling into the room like circus clowns, shouting 'What's wrong' and 'What is it?' and other clever remarks. Nothing, I told them. Bad dream. Because by then the host had turned back into his usual obsequious self.

Are you sure? they asked. My Mom gave me a searching look, and my Dad suggested maybe I should 'see someone'. Oh no, I told them. Nothing to worry about. Just fine, thanks. I hated the thought I might have to go back to that damn hospital. More important, I was scared. Too scared to talk about it or get help. Because seeing Paul on network TV did not strike me as all that different from strange sounds on the telephone or a shower that smelled of perfume. I could have called the emergency number the protection team had given me, but what would I do if they said they hadn't detected anything? I went to bed that night holding on tight to my protection and saying my formula over and over.

Paul didn't go away. Two days later I was walking on the old shopping street of our town when I saw a meter maid giving a ticket to a blue Mercedes. As I walked past her she glanced up from her pad – and Paul was looking right at me. I ran. I didn't wait for the meter maid to change back from my dead cousin in drag, I took off down the block, nearly knocking down an old lady who shouted after me. I didn't stop to help her or apologize. I was scared she'd turn into Paul.

That time I got as far as standing by the telephone, taking deep breaths and reciting Alison Birkett's home phone number over and over in my mind, like some deep meditation release chant. When I finally walked away without calling I almost had to laugh. At one time I would have loved an excuse to call her at home. But not that excuse.

The next day I had a date with my friend Barb to go to the park. The last thing I needed, I thought, was Barb going on about her latest catalogue of cute boys who'd asked her to some school ritual or something. I thought of cancelling, but I didn't want Barb attacking me. We'd been friends since second grade, and she'd been getting upset that since I became 'famous' I'd stopped seeing her.

We were walking down by the pond, with Barb doing all the talking and me nervously looking at everyone who passed, even dogs and squirrels, when a skateboarder spun by us. I didn't even notice him. I was looking the other way at a baby carriage. Suddenly Barb grabbed my arm. 'Ellen,' she said. 'That kid on that skateboard? He looked just like your cousin Paul.'

Barb will probably never know why I hugged her and kissed her and then ran off as fast as I could.

'Alison,' I shouted into the phone by the park restaurant. 'He's alive!'

Ms Birkett met my parents and me at the SDA headquarters in Manhattan. The protection team came too; it was the first time I'd seen them in weeks. I don't know what I expected, really. Maybe some great enactment to bring Paul back from the dead. What I got was tests. Though my folks made a weak protest, and I didn't like the idea at all, we let Ms Birkett convince us we had to get some scientific basis for what was going on. At least it wasn't like the hospital. They didn't strap me down or anything, and they did all the testing in a large open room with a carpet and couches.

As a government agency, the SDA displays portraits of the president in all their offices. You know the kind – an official government photo of our nation's leader smiling blankly in his official bird costume and sacred headdress, with painted-in guardian spirits hovering in the background, like Secret Service agents. In the middle of all their testing, when I realized none of it was going to do anything worse than bore me, I started looking around the room and my eyes clicked on the president's portrait. Paul was there. His face looked down at me from underneath the president's jewelled and feathered cap of office. 'There he is,' I told them. 'Right there. In that picture.'

They all stared and then a bunch of them ran over with their meters and gauges. By the time they'd reblessed their equipment the photo had changed back again, but that didn't stop them. After about ten minutes they announced 'Significant computational levels of post-manifestational residualism.' SDA people love talking like that.

They went back to me after that and tested me all the rest of the afternoon. Later, I found out they had sent teams to the various places and objects where I'd told them I'd seen Paul. At the end of the day they reported that early indications showed that the 'manifestations' were genuine (I figured that that meant I wasn't crazy)

and did not come from 'the enemy'. That was why the
protection teams hadn't picked up anything. They'd set
their monitors for Bright Beings only. The investigators
said they needed to do further tests and run computer
analyses, but I could go home.

Wait a minute, I told them. Go home? What did they
plan to do? Analyze. Examine. Ponder. Report in five
days. I jumped up and strode from the office. 'Ellen?'
Alison Birkett called, but I didn't turn. A moment later,
my folks came scurrying after me.

The week went more quickly than I thought it would.
Paul appeared twice – once as my school principal in the
middle of an assembly, the second time as a kid running
out of a store, with the store owner chasing him and
calling him a thief. I almost joined the chase, but I knew
it wouldn't do any good. Even if I'd caught him, he would
have changed back again.

Six days later (it took them an extra day) we were all
back there; me, my folks, Ms Birkett, her own team, the
SDA techs, and their boss, a real 'holycrat' as Alison
called such people. Only now two other people had come
along; government lawyers in their dark suits and short
haircuts. Alison had invited them. Summoned them was
more like it. Told them they would 'hear something vital
to our mutual concerns'. So they came and sat upright,
frowning at both the SDA and Alison Birkett, who
appeared very relaxed in an antique chair with curved
arms and a flared back. She wore a dark gold suit and
had her hair combed back from her face. Leaning back
in her chair she set her right elbow on the chair arms and
rested her chin in the bridge between her first and second
fingers. She looked the absolute model of fascination as
she listened to the techs explain what was happening.

It must have taken some doing even to *look* fascinated.
The whole thing was about me and Paul, but I still felt like
going to sleep. 'Transcendental biology' the SDA people
called it, a subject even more confusing to me than sacred

physics. What it came down to was this. When people die they take several weeks to really let go of their attachment to their bodies, or rather their memories of their bodies – 'the post-consciousness morphological field' as one of the techs put it. Once the dead person does that they suddenly discover their guide and off they go to the 'Whistling Land' as a deep meditation traveller once called the Place of the Dead.

This is the way it's supposed to work. Sometimes, however, if the death comes as too great a shock, the person gets jolted right out of his morphological field. And then he can get stranded, because by the time the guide shows up the person's spirit essence has wandered off and the guide can't smell where to find him. Not knowing what to do, the dead person tries to get back to the world of the living.

'But why me?' I asked. 'I mean, why does he appear just to me?'

'Well, we don't know that he does,' the holycrat said. 'Perhaps he manifests to others who simply fail to identify him.'

'Oh,' I said cleverly. 'I hadn't thought of that.'

'But in fact,' one of the techs said (his boss frowned at him, but he didn't seem to notice), 'detached spirits usually try to fix themselves to a significant figure from their past existence. The technical term for this is emoto-tropism.'

Another joined in, 'Don't forget, in several of the manifestations, such as the television programme, only Ellen perceived the anomalous presence.'

'Though not all,' said yet another. 'Let's not forget the presidential portrait. Or the incident with the skateboard.'

I wanted to ask how we could help Paul, but before I could speak Alison signalled to me to keep silent. She said, 'It looks like we might have a special opportunity here. A chance to act in the best interests of both my clients and the government.'

Later, after the meeting, Ms Birkett took my folks and me to a restaurant in Greenwich Village. While we ate lunch she explained what she had in mind. 'We could keep after them,' she said, 'but frankly, the lawsuit would take years. And believe me, the strain would not help you, and it certainly would not help Paul. He needs anchoring.'

My mother said, 'Can't they just release him? Maybe they can summon some sort of guide for him.'

'Perhaps,' Ms Birkett said. 'But maybe we can think of something else.' Sometimes, she said, the Bright Beings can raise up a human spirit.

Mom said, 'You mean Paul can become a Benign One?'

'Not exactly. But he can become a helper or a guardian.'

Dad said, 'And does that mean we just let the government off the hook?'

Ms Birkett said, 'Believe me, the scandal will not vanish just because we come to a settlement concerning our private suit. After all, we brought the suit to draw attention to the case. In that sense, it has served its purpose. Maybe the time has come for you to get back your lives.'

'I don't know,' Dad said.

'Let me put it this way,' Ms Birkett said. 'If it serves the politicians and the media to pursue this, they will do so with or without our suit. And if they decide it does not serve their purposes, they will let it quietly die away, no matter what we do to keep it alive.'

'What about Paul?' I asked. 'Doesn't anybody care what Paul wants?'

Alison nodded. 'Yes. Exactly. Ellen, Paul has attached himself to you. What do you think he would want? To go to the Place of the Dead – provided we could somehow arrange that, and I don't know that we can – or to find a fixed place here in the world?'

'I don't know,' I said, and could feel myself wanting to cry. 'I just don't know.'

She leaned forward slightly, and I think she might have taken my hand, or patted it, if my folks hadn't been there. 'I'm sorry,' she said, 'Maybe we all need some time to think.' I nodded, not looking at her.

Mom said, 'Perhaps you could investigate what we could get? For a settlement, I mean.'

'Certainly,' Ms Birkett said.

We left pretty soon after that. I don't think any of us cared very much about dessert. In the car, my folks argued most of the way home. Not about the case, or Paul, just dumb-things. Petty things. I thought, this has got to stop.

Over the next few days one thought came to me over and over – if only he would speak to me, if only I could ask him. The next time he appeared was on a TV commercial. Remember that beer company that used a dog as a mascot? Well, one evening they ran that commercial between a couple of sitcoms and the dog came out with Paul's face. 'Why don't you talk to me?' I said to the TV. 'How am I supposed to know what you want?' But then the commercial ended and he was gone.

The next time was in a fitting room in a department store. The ladies' fitting room. Paul replaced the elderly woman who counted how many items you were holding and gave you a plastic card with the number on it. Some poor woman noticed his young male face and gave a little shriek, but I paid no attention. 'I love you, Paul,' I said. 'Please tell me what we should do. Please.' He said nothing, just looked at me, with such sadness I realized that 'broken heart' was more than a corny cliché. I hurt, as if my heart had shattered in my chest.

'Did you want to try these on, Miss?' the woman asked, suddenly back in her body. I threw the clothes at her and ran out of the store.

When I phoned Alison at home she thanked me for calling. She hadn't wanted to push me, she said. She asked if I could come to her office.

'Shall I bring my folks?' I asked.

'If you like. But you might want to hear the terms yourself first.'

I went alone. My folks didn't expect me for several hours and I had my allowance for the train. When I got to her office she was wearing jeans and a man's shirt with the sleeves rolled up.

She said, 'I had a long talk with the government people. Several long talks, to be honest. We came to a tentative agreement. If you and your folks drop the suit, they will publicly admit culpability and pay damages of $750,000. They will also take on the cost of the independent team monitoring your protection.'

'What about Paul?' I said.

'And the Bright Beings have agreed to dissolve Lisa Black Dust 7. Completely dissolve her, as if she never existed.'

'What about Paul?' I repeated.

She was fiddling with something on her desk, a totem of some sort. I realized she didn't want to look at me. She said, 'Paul becomes – if we agree to the settlement – Paul becomes a guardian spirit.'

'Of what? He's got to be a guardian of *something*.' I never knew I could talk to her like that.

She sighed. 'Elevators,' she said. 'The Bright Beings have offered to make Paul the guardian spirit of elevators.'

I started to laugh. It wasn't funny. I just couldn't help myself. 'Elevators,' I said. 'Oh God, Paul. Elevators!'

3

So now you know. When you step into an elevator, that narrow steel pole that stands next to the door – the one with the dots for eyes and an oval for a mouth and strands of nylon at the top for hair – that's my cousin Paul. Or at least the 'husk' as they say at the SDA. The physical chamber for the spirit to inhabit. Do you touch it? Do you rub the steel or touch the mouth for good luck, for protection? If you ride an elevator on the way to a business appointment, do you kiss the pole and say something like, 'Blessed Spirit of this vehicle of ascent, carry me to victory with my new client'? Does it make you feel better?

I went to see him the other day. I went back to that building where he used to work, where he did whatever dumb stupid thing he did to attract the interest of Lisa Black Dust 7. I got in an elevator – there's a whole row but it doesn't matter which one, he inhabits all of them, in every building – and when it took off, and everyone who'd wanted to had touched the husk and stepped away, I went over to the pole and whispered, 'I'm sorry, Paul. I love you. I hope it's what you wanted.'

I don't know, but I think the face, the dots and the oval, glowed slightly. Just a little. Just for a moment.

When I got home that evening, I went to my room and dug something out from the back of the cabinet underneath my desk. My framed *Time* magazine cover of Alison Birkett. For a while I just held it in my hands and looked at it. I should just throw it away, I thought. What's the point of keeping it there, under my yearbooks and my old report cards? Throw it away. But I didn't. Instead, I hugged it to my chest and lay down on my bed, with my knees drawn up against my arms. And I cried. I cried for Paul, I cried for Alison. Most of all, I guess, I cried for me.

Part Two

BENIGN ADJUSTMENTS

I pray that love may never come to me
with murderous intent,
in rhythms measureless and wild.

Euripides

1

So there it is. Paul and Alison and me. And of course, Lisa Black Dust 7. Last night, I got out that old manuscript. It took me a while to find it. I'd buried it pretty well and for a few minutes I even thought I must have thrown it out. But no, there it was, along with my high school yearbook, the photo from my senior tattoo initiation – and that damn *Time* magazine cover. Alison Birkett, frozen in time, just like the corpse of Rebecca Rainbow under glass in the New York Stock Exchange.

I sat down and read it through, and I guess I didn't cringe more than fifty or sixty times. What the hell, like I said back then, I was just a kid, right? Me and Alison. Shit. I can remember it so sharply, sitting there in her office, just about levitating with excitement. When I decided to write all this down, everything that's just happened, I thought I probably should go back over the old stuff and edit it. Do a little cleaning up with the added wisdom of ten more years stuck on the planet. But now that I've read it, I think I'll just leave it like it is. Somehow, I feel I owe it to Paul not to change anything, to keep the feelings the way they were when I wrote them down. And maybe I also owe it to Alison. I'm not sure about that. I don't think I'm ever sure of anything when it comes to me and Alison Birkett.

It's hard to know where to begin. Or maybe I'm just

scared. I was going to start with the rally in Miracle Park, but maybe the real beginning was earlier, when Joan Monteil and I went to a Bead Woman for a Speaking at the start of our 'relationship'. It was Joan's idea. After several weeks of Joan hanging around, bringing me cute little toys, inviting me to openings and play readings, telling me how great I looked in whatever I happened to wear (I considered trying on more and more bizarre outfits, such as covering myself in bandages, or Victorian dresses stapled all over with baseball cards, just to see what she would say), when I finally gave in and went to bed with her, she was so overwhelmed she insisted we go see an SDA certified Speaker the very next day.

I didn't want to tell Joan what I thought of SDA certifications. Or Bead Workers, for that matter. But that was no criticism of her. I didn't talk about stuff like that with anyone. So there was Joan, sitting on the edge of her wooden chair with red and yellow beads caught in her hair from where the woman poured them over her head, and me doing my best to stare out at 7th Avenue through all the ancestral statues, offering stones and other junk hung in the window, and wishing I could shake out the beads still stuck in *my* hair, without that SDA certified malpractitioner scolding me for 'pruning the Tree of the Ancients' when suddenly the woman grabs my shoulders in her certified hands and kisses me on my forehead and above my heart.

'What are you doing?' I shouted, and jumped back so hard I almost upped the damn tree right out of its roots.

The Speaker only smiled happily at me, but Joan said, 'Ellen! Don't you know what that was? That was the Kiss of the Beloved.'

'I *know* that.'

'Well,' Joan burbled on, 'it means something really wonderful has come into your life.' Her voice didn't leave any doubt as to what she considered was the well spring of the divine beneficence. As for myself, I don't think I carcd much what the source of my good fortune might be (at least I was pretty sure it wasn't Joan Monteil). I just wanted to leave. 'I don't need any fresh wonders,' I said. 'My life is fine the way it is.'

The Speaker looked at me ponderously for a moment, trying for professional significance I guess, then back down at the various coloured beads scattered on the tabletop's ornate grid. 'Look,' she said, and stuck a finger out towards two large beads, one gold, one black, each resting on the borderline between sections of the grid. 'Sister Night and Sister Bright are swimming towards each other. And look, here's an underground river bursting into the day.' She pointed to a wavy line of blue beads near the centre of the table, where a painting of the Sun appeared.

'I said I'm fine, okay?' I said. 'The Supreme Court ruled you can't do this. It violates privacy for a Speaker to give unsolicited predictions. Harrison vs. Truesource Center of Revelations.'

Joan's eyes widened even further at this new revelation of my resources. Ellen Pierson – artist, seducer and legal scholar. Any more excitement and Joan's eyes would pop out, like fresh beads to disturb the reading.

The Speaker said quietly, 'A bad judgement, though of course predicted by those of us in the profession. It will not stand long. Free speech will take precedence. At any rate, may I remind you that you did indeed seek me for a consultation. I did not come banging on your door at six in the morning.'

I told her, 'Well now I'm withdrawing my authorization.'

The Speaker said, 'Why are you wearing protection?'

I jerked my glance down to where my hand was touching the medallion I still wore underneath my shirt. I let my hand drop. I couldn't think of anything to say. The Bead Woman closed her eyes and grimaced slightly, as if squinting inside herself for some gem of knowledge lying in a jumble of prophetic images. She opened her eyes to look at me warily. 'You have a chip in your body,' she said, with a touch of amazement. I glanced at the doorway, wondering if it contained hidden scanners which would have reported such information to her before she came out to meet us.

'Wow,' Joan said, 'a chip?'

'Forget it,' I told her. 'It's dead.'

'But what's it for? Are you a spy or something?'

'It's a family heirloom,' I said. Leaning over, I shook the remaining beads loose from my hair.

The Speaker said, 'I'm afraid it's too late to force-alter the configurations.'

'I'm not trying to alter anything,' I told her. 'I'm trying to leave.' As I strode out Joan came scurrying after me.

'Ellen?' she said. 'Honey?' I think I growled. 'What's wrong? I thought it sounded great. What she said, I mean.'

I stopped in front of a chilli parlour, by a sign promising that every bowl of chilli was blessed by the spirit remnants of dead Native precursors. 'Joan,' I said, trying to sound vaguely warm and promising, 'I need some time alone. I hope you can understand that.'

'Oh,' she said. 'Oh, of course.' I hurried away before she could change her mind.

When I got home I sat down in the old wingback chair, pink with little white flowers, I'd somehow managed to get all the way from my parents' house to my minimal (not minimalist) apartment overlooking 2nd Avenue. Somehow, I found myself sad, like I wanted to cry and couldn't think of why. I tried to make myself excited, amused, angry about Joan, but none of these got me anywhere. Looking around the room I noticed Nora and Toby, the stuffed totem animals who had come with me (and the chair) from Long Island to the city. Plump little lions, they sat on their hind legs on top of the bookcase my carpenter friend Sharon had made for me during our brief affair. Toby and Nora were pressing their front paws together in a Circle of Invocation. I watched them for a while, telling myself I could see, or at least sense, the energy passing between them, rising and falling with the beating of the Earth. I loved my two seven-inch friends. I hadn't kept very many relics from my childhood. Most of my childhood tools of power now lay in a sanctified remembrance box in the family shrine down in the rec room of my folks' house. I smiled, remembering how I'd cried during my puberty rites when the Teller had used her red cord to transfer the power into more appropriate, more adult, vessels. But not Nora and Toby. They were staying with me and that was that.

I walked over to them, smiling, and stroked their soft golden backs. 'What do you think, girls?' I said. 'Is my underground river about to burst into the light of day?' I didn't dare pick them up. The river of tears would burst its underground banks.

This is ridiculous, I told myself. She predicted something good. What was I so upset about? I needed something to do. I decided to call my friend Harry and tell him about how I'd surrendered to Joan. If I hadn't given up the idea of 'best friends' when I was fourteen, Harry Astin would have been it.

Harry edits a weekly newspaper for the metalworking 'community', as they like to call themselves, a job which allows him to use journalist jargon, run occasional pieces on 'alchemy in the modern world' and stay alive while he assembles found poetry out of speeches by prominent Tellers spliced with headlines from newspaper tabloids, an art which twice has brought him close to charges of blasphemy. Harry dresses in a style he calls 'Barney's drag', after an expensive clothing store. Though he never actually buys anything there, Harry visits Barney's often. He claims he once saw Martin Greenflower, the head of the New York College of Tellers and a prime source of material for Harry, blessing a rack of suits, probably in exchange for a kickback, or maybe a flattering dummy in Barney's yearly Rising of the Light window display.

'Ellen!' Harry said in his exaggerated Southern drawl. I could just see him waving his 'prosthetic cigarette' at the air. Harry's cigarette is one of those things I love about him. Originally part of a kit to help people stop smoking, the plastic glows red on one end when you suck on the other. Harry uses it as a prop to go with his swept-back blond hair and his pinstripe suits. 'I was just planning on asking the Benign Ones to guide my finger as I dialled you. What are you doing this afternoon?'

'Speaking to you, darling,' I said. 'Begging the Beings to lift me from my wearisome life.' Harry and I talked like that sometimes. Sorry.

'Wonderful. Then you can take my arm and stroll with me to Miracle Park. Alexander Timmerman has announced an enactment and no doubt stirring speech for three o'clock.'

'Great,' I said, meaning it. 'Is Glorybe coming?' Harry's girlfriend was named Gloria Roberta Feinstein, but ever since the first time they had made love Harry had called her 'Glorybe'.

'No,' Harry said, 'my dimmed Glory sits chained to her research module.'

'All the more reason for her to hear Timmerman speak on Liberation in the Age of Reform.'

It feels strange to write about Timmerman in such a casual way. People reading this may not have heard of my part in everything that happened, but they sure will remember Great Brother Alex. Back then, however, he was only an occasional curiosity on the evening news.

Harry and I met in front of the Spiritual Supply shop on 9th Street by 1st Avenue. Harry was wearing a light blue suit and a red and black striped tie. As I approached, Harry took a fake puff on his cigarette, held between two stiff fingers like a victory salute, then drew his hand away to blow imaginary smoke at me. It was only when he gave me the blue Timmerman button that I realized he was wearing one himself. He must have chosen the suit for the button to blend with the material.

Walking to the rally we saw pictures and totem statues of Alexander Timmerman in many of the store windows. A dress store featured a mannequin with Timmerman's head, including a pretty good copy of his famous head-dress, a beaded cap going down over the eyes and nose with multi-coloured beads in the shape of a bird across the forehead, and actual feathers coming down over the nose for the tail. Other than the mask, the dummy wore a sequin-splattered crepe de chine dress which matched the headdress nicely, but would have looked awful on Timmerman's squat weightlifter's body. A few doors down, an old bakery run by a mixture of Chinese and Russian immigrants proudly displayed a poppyseed almond cake in the shape of a man spreadeagled (or else doing jumping jacks), which Harry described as 'Brother Alex leaping to our rescue'.

As we approached the rally in Miracle Park (full name, Miguel Miracle of the Green Earth Recreational Area, but no one ever calls it that), we could hear loudspeakers blaring Timmerman's anthem, *Touching The Future*, with its never-ending refrain, 'If not now, when? If not here, where? And if not us, who? If not us, who?' Harry said, 'One almost expects to see a chorus line of owls.' Closer to the park, the crowd looked to be about a few hundred people – a mixture of students, yuppies on their lunch break (or out of work), a few drug dealers, some old Eastern Europeans, scattered tourists, and of course, the homeless, whose collective title always makes them sound like a tribe even when they're not.

Miracle Park was a homeless haven despite all the efforts of the police to exorcise them. In the early morning you could see middle-aged men and women and runaway kids curled up on the benches under the small shell which was supposed to be for bands but never was. I remember once when I couldn't sleep, going down to the park and seeing two kids with shaved heads and torn shirts which looked like they came from one of those paramilitary academies, like the Latterday Army of the Saints. The kids were holding a pair of thin foam mattresses, rolled up as if they were too precious to stretch them out on the dewy ground, and they were whispering and giggling, with the park lamps lighting up tattoos from homecoming enactments on the top of their heads. I stood there and thought how they weren't much older than I had been when all that stuff happened. When Paul got taken. And I remember thinking, now here I was, Paul's age. Except I would get older and Paul would stay the same, forever. I just about ran from the park, with the kids laughing behind me, probably thinking I was some straight who wanted to do an offering of protection against losing her home and finding herself in the tribe.

So there would have been homeless in Miracle Park no matter what. But in fact, Timmerman rallies always drew homeless people, from his first speeches back in New Chicago. Maybe you remember how the police tried to chase them off, and Timmerman shouted at the cops to 'let my brothers and sisters touch the living fire of hope.' That line, and the footage of the shabby people reaching up to the stage to touch the Beautiful Ones, the famous still photo of a gnarled diseased hand in a tattered glove reaching up for perfect fingers, these more than anything, were what made Timmerman famous.

Timmerman's detractors – 'professional cynics' he called them – claimed that the blessing of the homeless at his rallies was stage-managed, a fake. They pointed out how few homeless people actually showed up, and implied that Timmerman's 'operatives' spread the word on the street that crowds would not be welcome and the drunks and crazies especially should just stay away. I don't know. Until I got involved, I didn't care enough to investigate. Then later, things just got too complicated.

It was true that that day Harry and I didn't see more than fifty or sixty homeless people in the small crowd. They'd set up a shrine, though, off on the side. Not a bad job. They'd made a frame with pieces of wood and pipe and some crates and cardboard boxes. They'd decorated it with scraps of paper, bird feathers, bottle caps and a couple of rolls of toilet paper draped as streamers. Marker-drawn pictures of Miguel Miracle of the Green Earth (plus a couple of Rebecca Rainbow, for prosperity, and even one of Li Ku Unquenchable Fire, maybe for defiance), some drawn on paper bags or sheets of newspapers, were thumbtacked to the frame. Some had sayings and invocations, in English, Spanish or Russian, written over the eyes and mouth. In the shrine's centre, on a little wooden platform, stood a sanctified dollhouse. Judging from the broken pieces and the stains, the enactors probably found it on the street. Probably some stockbroker decided to get a fancier model in the hopes of moving up to a townhouse, and had thrown away the spirit aid which had brought him to where he was now. I wondered if a model home kept its certified SDA sanctification if you found it on the street. I wondered if an SDA sanctification meant anything even when you got it right from the store.

The homeless people who'd made the shrine didn't seem to share my doubts. They'd drawn arrows outside the shrine to the open room in the centre, which they'd filled with representations, some of them actual dolls (a few looked old enough to have survived since childhood) and some just twigs or cardboard cutouts. I imagined the ceremony, maybe late at night, with all the park people chanting together as they marched their proxies from the cold outdoors into the spiritual warmth of the dollhouse. Around the outside of the whole shrine I noticed the blackened dust left over after burning a large amount of flash powder. You never saw that at home when I was growing up. Any time we did a family enactment my mother got out the vacuum cleaner almost before we'd finished the chants and gestures for 'sealing the future'. I think that Mom believed that leaving a mess destroyed the power of the enactment.

Amid the ashes in the park I saw small deposits of unburned powder. Probably got wet, I thought, until it occurred to me that maybe they pissed on it. Some people believe that urine around the border of a shrine truly raises it to the level of true ground. Separates it from its entanglement in everyday reality. My mother preferred vacuum cleaners.

Standing there, I remembered something I'd seen once. It was right after Paul's ascent to guardianship (yes, I know the usual term is 'elevation', but I don't think that would go too well in this instance). Right after I stopped seeing Alison. I had gotten that feeling I sometimes got those days, that I couldn't breathe in my parents' house. It was late at night, and I put on some clothes and rushed outside. Once beyond the door my lungs started to work again, but I hurried away, just in case my father should wake up (I had just read how Malignant Ones sometimes provoked a man's prostate to compel him to piss in the middle of the night).

So I went for a walk, nervous that the police might spot me and shoo me back. But instead of a cop car trolling the development, I heard a kind of low growl, and when I came around the corner (Stairway-Joining-Heaven-and-Earth Drive) I saw something very strange, even after what had gone on over the past months. Three naked women, their bodies and faces streaked with mud (or maybe shit) were squatting in the road, humming or chanting, and urinating on some kind of white maze they'd drawn on the blacktop. In the centre of the maze lay a doll made of glass and carved crystal. I couldn't tell the women's ages. Their bodies looked lumpy, either from muscle or fat. When I first saw them I thought of nothing but, how could they get away with that on the North Shore of Long Island? And then sadness, or maybe shame, took hold of me as I thought of the puny enactments I had done for Paul, never even naked, let alone peeing in the street, and no wonder nothing I'd done had ever worked.

Then I became scared. Maybe they weren't women at all. Maybe Lisa's friends had come to get me. Grabbing hold of my talisman, I prayed that the chips in me were broadcasting to the right places while I recited my personal formula. They did turn and look at me. But instead of showing their teeth, like Lisa Black Dust 7, they just smiled. And – I'm not sure of this part, because it feels like I dreamed it or something – they blew kisses at me. What I am sure of is the sweet smell of flowers and the feeling of safety, so powerful I felt like I could howl and cry all night long. I didn't. What I did was run. I ran home as fast as I could.

I did my best to push the whole thing out of my mind. I used schoolwork, TV, gossip, and even an obnoxious boy named Johhny Olden, who believed he was in love with me. I thought about it, sometimes. Like when I had to pee. And once, during a Girls' Enactment after gym class, I found myself wondering what Ms Cohen would do if I dropped my shorts and peed at the foot of the Virginity Guardian. In a few weeks, however, I banished it so successfully I didn't think of it again. Until that day in Miracle Park.

Harry saved me from brooding. Puffing on his pc, he said, 'If this circus doesn't take off soon, perhaps we could sue Alexander in Consumer's Court.' I grinned, thinking of Timmerman as the first defendant in the special legal system he himself was proposing.

'He's a strange mixture, isn't he?' I said.

'As long as he amuses,' Harry said.

'No, really. Sometimes he acts like he wants to bring back the Revolution, and other times he just spends all his energy on food labels, mattress fillings, and windshield wipers.'

'Maybe his mother told him that genius lies in the details.'

Finally, the blaring music stopped. Everyone turned to the van parked at the end of the enactment area. Either Timmerman's divine Helpers or some clever lighting system was making the snakes glow and the sunwheel spin. 'They're hypnotizing us,' Harry said. 'The next time we go into a voting booth, we'll all start clucking like chickens.' Someone behind us shushed him. He blew imaginary smoke into the air.

A man and a woman came out of the van and started circling the stage area, making wide sweeping gestures with their arms. They were caked in mud, giving their bodies a look of ancient grey deserts. Harry whispered to me, 'Let's hope it doesn't start raining before they complete their performance.' This time, I shushed him. On top of the mud the men and women had pasted (I guess) dollar bills, advertising circulars, street handouts for discos and discount stores, and pictures of smiling women holding their breasts with 900 numbers across the nipples.

When they'd completed their circle, they stepped back to stand a little way apart facing the audience. With a loud grunt they crashed their hands together like cymbals – and burst into flames. All over their bodies the paper and mud were burning, while the two stood impassively, their hands clasped and their heads bent forward, like the people you sometimes see in government office buildings, hired to promote a spiritual atmosphere. Except these people were on fire.

I admit I gasped with everyone else, except Harry who kept his cool. 'Think they'll give me a light?' he said, holding up his pc, but I was straining to look through the cheering whistling crowd to see if I could spot the flame-proof bodysuit and the gas jets underneath the mud. Behind me someone said proudly, 'How about that? That's better than those horses he used in Boston. Only in New York, huh?'

The crowd cheered again, for there was Alex Timmerman, stepping through the double pillars of consumer fire, dressed, as always, in his enactment mask and a grey business suit. While the flames died down on his escorts, leaving them a mess of melting mud, Timmerman launched into his speech, an incongruous array of charges of corruption against government, corporations, and lobbyists, lacing it all with sensible proposals. He spoke of resanctifying our daily lives, of ways in which packagers drain divine nutrients from the food we eat, of banks and lawyers and congressmen in 'a black hole of greed, sucking in money and information, never to be seen again'. He talked of raising up our sexual selves to levels of selfless love and power. In short, he was all over the map. There was a curious excitement about the speech, as if everything he said was something you'd once thought about for yourself. But if the crowd was excited it wasn't because of Timmerman's ideas or proposals. Speech-making wasn't what they had come for.

How does someone get one, let alone two, Devoted Ones to act as his private agents of benediction? Getting Malignant Ones to work for you isn't all that difficult. Gluttons that they are, they'll arrange your partner's death, or your boyfriend's slavish devotion, or maybe just some premature promotions in your career, all in exchange for the thrill of tasting human nastiness and degradation. But you can't hire Benign Ones at your local temp agency. 'The Devoted Ones lift you gently, the Ferocious Ones knock you down with a club.' Usually, if a Benign One appears at all in someone's life it does so briefly, at a time of crisis, and mostly in disguise, like the taxi driver who showed up at just the right moment to rescue Ingrid Burning Snake from the sec police in the early days of the Revolution. Or they counteract some Malignant intervention, like the waitress who tripped and spilled coffee on the supposed travelling salesman who was hypnotizing Governor

Chichester to keep her from reaching the presidential debate studio.

So how did Timmerman manage it? Fasting? Enactments in dark caves, or the desert, to purify his purpose, 'expunging self from the equation of his actions'? Or did the Devoted Ones, his 'choir of angels' as the press called them, attach themselves to his campaign for their own inscrutable purposes?

Two figures walked out from the audience and turned to stand alongside Alex Timmerman. 'Oh my God!' a woman in front of me shrieked. 'He was standing right next to me. I could have touched him!' They appeared as a man and a woman, though as far as anyone knew the categories didn't mean anything to Bright Beings. Just shells of appearance. The man wore a suit, grey like Timmerman's, with a red tie loosened at the neck. The woman wore a skirt and blouse and running shoes, like those office workers who keep their high heels in their desks (I found myself wondering if she'd modelled herself after women seen only in the street). Their faces and hands gleamed with a light that first flickered, then gleamed in intensity, as if they'd turned up a rheostat. At the same time, their faces drained of expression until they looked like mannequins in a department store.

With a roar that made me wince, the crowd all chanted together, 'Devoted Ones, we thank you for your devotion. We know that nothing we have done deserves your precious intervention.' And then they began to push forward, everyone hoping to touch the Spirits, palm to palm, finger to finger. It was all I could do to stay upright.

The only other person not moving was Harry. 'You're not fighting to be blessed,' I told him.

He shrugged gently. 'I might tear my suit.' He didn't ask my excuse.

I stopped paying attention to Harry or the Benign Ones and their would-be recipients because of someone else who had caught my eye. A woman stood a few feet behind Timmerman, her arms crossed, her body bent slightly backwards as if she was leaning against an invisible tree. Short, about five feet three inches, with completely black hair, straight, combed forward in front and cut short on the sides, she looked like someone I might have met at The Unfertilized Egg, my favourite cruising bar. She was wearing a loose black turtleneck tucked into close-fitting black jeans with a wide silver belt and dark red cowboy boots. She'd put the boots on over the pants' legs, which in the Egg would have signalled a fem, or at least not a butch. Her thick makeup would have made the point more loudly. She'd done her eyes in heavy black liner, giving them a deep hollow look. Either she was naturally pale or had made her face up white, with no blusher, but dark red lipstick.

She was just standing there, just watching the crowd and the Benign Ones working the audience like an auctioneer at an estate sale. But something about her made me forget the noise and the pushing, Timmerman's crowing about 'the life and truth of the people', even Froggy 1 and Froggy 2 (don't ask me why I called Our Devoted Friends that, maybe from the way they hopped back and forth in front of the mob). 'Harry?' I said. He made a noise. 'Who's that? Behind Timmerman.'

'Timmerman's publicist?' he said. 'His downtown liaison? His polltaker and sacred performance artist?'

'I don't know,' I said.

Finally, marshals came out to escort the divine guests away from the crowd. Though a few people shouted that they hadn't had their turn, that it wasn't fair and what about their rights, Timmerman quieted them down through platitudes about spreading the power through devoted humans. Or maybe it wasn't such a platitude. The people who'd been touched seemed compelled to touch others. They kept putting their hands on each other, or hugging, or rubbing against each other, sliding and lifting, sometimes kissing, sometimes moving their hands along each other's backs or thighs. It was sexual and very overt, yet very innocent, as if . . . as if nothing was expected to come of it. Most of our touching, even necking, locks into a context of messages, like 'This is going to lead to screwing', or 'This is not going to lead to screwing', or 'Now we have a real relationship', or 'Not this time, or the next, but the time after that.'

These people reminded me of the three-year-old son of a friend of mine, who after I'd taken a shower and was wearing his mother's bathrobe, came up and put a hand straight on my crotch, saying, 'What you got there?' There was no message in the touching, just the excitement of contact. And yet, there was an intensity, a kind of burning under the surface, that was both exciting and frightening.

Mostly they touched each other, and it didn't matter if it was a student, or a yuppie, or some homeless kid whose clothes and body stank. They just wanted to touch, to kiss. But they also reached out to those who hadn't received the blessing, and while some drew back, others laughed, a little embarrassed, but joined in, like housewives finding themselves in a group sex enactment and discovering that once they've got the paint and the little bells on, and slashed their clothes, and set the cakes on fire, and started faceless screwing, that they like it and why have they never done this before?

And it wasn't just people they touched. A few of them would stroke or rub against the trees, even kissing the branches, the way you might kiss down the length of your lover's arm. One person was sliding her body along the length of a park bench. Another bent down to reach for a squirrel. When the squirrel ran away from him, he just made circles on the blacktop with his hands spread wide, as if to take in as much surface as possible.

Harry said something about Timmerman and brotherhood, but I wasn't listening. I felt strange watching them.

There weren't really that many; maybe twenty or thirty who'd actually received the touch. 'Something's going on,' I thought. I remember those words, the sentence forming in my mind. And then I looked at the woman standing behind Timmerman. She hadn't moved, she just stood there, with her black-rimmed eyes looking vaguely across the crowd. For a moment I thought she was looking at me. I jerked my head back, closed my eyes and opened them again. Her gaze had shifted.

Timmerman was talking about human liberation and economics, citing statistics and trends along with his slogans, and it really did seem like people were listening, paying attention. Not noticing all that *touching*, all those people rubbing against each other, against lamp posts and garbage cans. I felt clumsy, like I had too many arms and legs and no idea where to put them. Two women, very tall, wearing nylon wigs, were passing money back and forth, sliding it against parts of their bodies and laughing, not just the official sexual parts, though certainly those too, but elbows, behind the knees, around the wrists, the small of the back, touching everywhere like a whip drawn slowly back and never cracked . . .

I've got to get out of here, I thought. Somewhere soft where I could think. Soft? I thought of Harry, but instead of telling him we had to go I just imagined the cold tip of his prosthetic cigarette climbing slowly up my spine. In the front of the crowd a man had taken off his shirt and jacket and was sliding his necktie all over his upper body. A child had turned the jacket inside out and put it on, hugging the fabric against herself. Everyone was smiling, moaning, while Alex Timmerman told them about consumer fraud and children's spirit vocalizations, leveraged buyouts and sacred agonies of democratic change. I wanted to look at Harry and didn't dare, certain he would slide against me and start pulling my hair, slowly pulling my head back . . .

And then the voice came. 'Ellen?' it said. 'Ellen Pierson?'

She might as well have shoved me, as hard as she could. I felt grateful and angry, grateful she'd pulled me loose from Timmerman's cadres, furious that it had to be her, that it wasn't Harry, or just my own will. Why hadn't I left? Why couldn't I have stayed home? Or gone off with Joan? How did I look? Could she have been anything? Was I sweating? Would she see it in my face if I turned around? Could I just walk away, maybe move into the crowd, as if I needed to hear Timmerman more clearly? Maybe I could abandon dignity and run like hell.

I turned around. My relief astonished me when I saw she didn't look old. A few more lines but hardly any grey hairs. More casual clothes than years ago – a blue silk zipper jacket over a pale yellow blouse and pleated pants belted with a gold weave cloth belt. Her hair looked softer, not as chic as I remembered (though how could I trust my fourteen-year-old just-a-kid sensibility?). Cut fairly short, brushed back along the sides. And her figure hadn't changed, no sloppiness or sagging. Probably worked out in a gym, I thought, and could hardly believe my own nastiness. I didn't dare think what I looked like. I'd sure as hell changed a lot more in the last thirteen years than she had.

'Alison,' I said. 'Hello.' Silence. Behind me, the loudspeakers blared Timmerman speaking about hospitals and spiritual malpractice. I could hear laughter and drawn-out sighs and knew that the blessed were still touching each other and everything else they could reach. It no longer mattered much (except that I discovered I wanted to talk about it with her, get her opinion).

Harry's hand waving his pc stopped me from trying to think of something to say. 'Oh,' I said. 'Um, Harry, this is Alison Birkett. Alison, this is Harry Astin.' I added, 'Alison's an old friend. Of my family.' I didn't know why I said that, only that I didn't dare look at her for fear I would start blushing.

Harry bowed slightly. I had no idea if the name had

registered. I'd never told Harry about my brief time as a celebrity, my 'fifteen minutes in the centre of the story' as people say. I'd thought about telling him. If anyone, it would have been Harry. But then I always decided that if he didn't know about Paul and everything else, I didn't want to pop my bubble of a normal life. But Harry still might have known Alison Birkett's name. For that matter he might have known my whole history and just respected my reticence.

He sucked on his pc until it glowed and then waved it grandly towards Timmerman and the crowd. When I looked I noticed that the woman with the black ringed eyes had left. Harry said, 'Quite a party.'

Alison said, 'Indeed it is, Mr Astin.'

Smiling, with what he called his 'toothy charm' Harry asked, 'Are you a sister, Ms Birkett? Or just a tourist, like Ellen and me?'

With a somewhat thinner smile back she said, 'Oh, I'm definitely a visitor and not a partaker. Though maybe a little more than a tourist. I seem to have attended quite a few of Mr Timmerman's rallies lately.' Something about the comment, or the voice, sent a small shock through me.

Harry said, 'So I gather the choir of angels has not sung to you?'

Alison's smile opened wider. 'No,' she said, 'I'm afraid I haven't sought the divine touch. And what about you? You're not seizing your chance to gaze into paradise?'

Harry waved his cigarette. 'I'm sure Ellen will tell you I have enough trouble seeing my own face in the mirror.'

None of us said anything for a moment, while behind me Timmerman seemed to be finishing his speech. Finally, Alison said, 'You look wonderful, Ellen. How have you been?'

'Fine.'

'I'm really glad to hear that. It's been almost ten years, hasn't it?'

'Seven,' I said. Silence again. Neither of us was going to mention our last meeting when I marched into her office and demanded she show me how to deactivate the chips stuck in my body. I would take my chances, I told her. I didn't want her or the SDA watching over me.

Harry said, 'Well, I guess I better return to my work, such as it is.'

When Harry had left, Alison said, 'I'm glad I ran into you, Ellen.'

'Are you?'

She ignored my rudeness. 'May I buy you a cup of coffee? Now that I see you, I realize there's something I would like to discuss with you.'

'Sure,' I said. As we left the park I glanced back at the remains of the rally. The woman was back, talking now to Timmerman who stood holding his helmet under his arm, like some ghost carrying his chopped-off head as he wanders the streets.

We didn't say much as we walked. I asked about her practice and she said she'd been limiting it to private civil cases. She asked, 'What sort of work did you pursue? Or do you mind my asking? I can withdraw the question.'

'Of course not,' I said. I considered lying to see how she'd react, but couldn't think of anything fast enough. 'I'm a graphic artist,' I said. 'Advertising logos, political posters, sometimes even my own pictures.' She asked some questions about my work, about individual style and commercial demands, grades of materials, working to deadlines, how much was done by computer, copyright and trademark issues. They were reasonable questions, much better than my terse answers.

'What did you think of that shrine?' she asked. 'The one in the park.'

I shrugged. 'I assumed some homeless people made it.'

'That was my guess. I liked it. It seemed more creative than those huge expensive things put up in Central Park every summer.'

'Then it's good you got to see it,' I said. 'The Park Police'll probably make them take it down after the rally.'

'Yes, of course. I wonder,' she said. 'I wonder if it helps them. The homeless people, I mean. I wonder if their devotion to Alexander Timmerman helps them.'

'Well,' I said, 'His Benevolent Friends certainly seem to make them feel happy. At least while they're around.'

'Yes. Yes, you got that impression, didn't you?'

We went to the Rogue Elephant, one of those East Village coffee shops in what used to be basement apartments, where everything is brown walls, wooden tables, wrought-iron chairs, loud music, and lots of people talking about texts, landlords, relationships and recent sessions with their inner healers. We sat down at the back, next to a board with hooks for keys to the toilets.

When I'd ordered cappuccino and Alison had ordered mint tea, she said to me, 'I really am glad to see you.' I wanted to say, 'Then isn't this your lucky day?' but managed to stop myself. She said, 'You look so much like yourself, Ellen. I know that's a terrible thing to say, but I can't think of how else to put it.'

'And you hardly look a day older yourself,' I said, and wished I hadn't.

Our drinks came. We reached into the bowl of Founder's Dust next to the sugar and chemical sweeteners, and sprinkled a few grains over the mugs. Having transformed the liquids from dead pieces of plant soaked in water into food, we each said a silent sanctification before we lifted them to our mouths. My sanctification was quite simple really. Something like, 'Get me through this without screaming or crying. Please.'

After I'd sipped my coffee I leaned back and said, 'So how did you find me, Alison? Credit checks? Tapping into Sacred Revenue Service computer files? Or did you have detectives triangulating reports of my whereabouts?'

She smiled. 'Much simpler, I'm afraid. It was the chip.

Not mine, the SDA's. I know you deactivated both of them, but all SDA chips give off a lifelong tracer signal on the original frequency.'

Sonofabitch, I thought to myself. Just let your government get its claws on you. I wondered if the Speaker had picked the signal up on a scanner. I said, 'Leave it to our guardians never to pass up an opportunity.'

'Precisely,' Alison Birkett said, and smiled at me.

I knew I should have been angry that she'd played a game on me, stage-managing our coincidental meeting. But somehow, I just felt, well, proud that I'd seen through her. And that I knew she'd expected me to. As if she'd set the game up for both of us and invited me to join in with her. But if I felt that, I certainly wasn't going to let her know that I did.

'I'll be right back,' I said, and grabbed the key to the ladies' room from above my head. When I got inside the tiny cracked cubicle I took a deep breath, then squinted into the foggy chipped mirror. Do you ever find yourself wanting to impress someone and thinking, 'Why do I care?' This was Alison Birkett, the woman who'd promised to protect my cousin and then let the snakes get him. The woman who said we'd roast the SDA until they shrivelled up and then sold Paul out for guardian of goddamn elevators. Ms 'Just leave it to me, Ms Pierson.' Ms 'You and me together, Ellen, we'll take on the whole United States Government *and* the Living World.' Shit.

I splashed some water on my hands and ran them through my hair, hoping the damp would spring some curl back to life. Damn beauty parlour, I thought. They'd promised me that the perm was not only all natural but charged with the energy of Mirando Glowwood, who'd been a hairdresser before his Awakening as a Founder.

I found a lipstick in my jeans pocket, drew a line on each cheek and rubbed them smooth, then did my lips, after which I blotted and rubbed most of it off, so the colour wouldn't stand out too much. At least, I thought,

I've still got my 'strong nose and high energy cheekbones', as my ex, Elinor, used to say.

Back at the table, Alison sat with hands folded on the tabletop, firm enough to keep the table from floating away should the Founders return and cancel gravity, like they did in the battle of New Chicago. She smiled at me, looking *so* happy to see me, as if we'd only drifted apart due to our busy schedules. Probably I was imagining it, but it looked to me like she'd combed her hair.

I sat down and sipped the cappuccino. Making my voice stern, I said, 'So why *did* you want to see me?'

'There's something going on,' she said. 'Something with Timmerman. And it's nasty.'

'Nasty how?' I had visions of stern mistresses in bird helmets running spanking parlours for government officials at Consumer Liberation headquarters.

'At least one death,' Alison said. 'One I know of.'

'A death?' I repeated.

'Last month, in Seattle, a man named Jack Chikowsky was trampled to death by a group of about ten people, apparently in a highly charged state of sexual ecstasy. According to witnesses, the victim was a willing participant, having stripped naked and covered himself with mud before lying on the ground in front of the dancers. Police reports state that none of the group knew Chikowsky or even each other. Nor did they exactly remember what they had done.'

'Well,' I said, 'at least he died happy.'

Alison said, 'Jack Chikowsky was a friend of mine, Ellen. He and I lived together for a while when we were both in law school. We'd stayed friends ever since.'

'I'm sorry,' I told her, looking down at the table. And then I couldn't help myself. Taking a sip of my coffee, I said, 'At least it wasn't like he was your cousin or something.'

Alison sighed. She looked down at the table, more hurt, or maybe embarrassed, than angry.

Goddamn you, I thought. *You* expect *me* to be perfect? 'I'm sorry,' I told her. 'It was a cheap shot. And I'm sorry your friend died.'

'There's more,' she said. 'I'd been hearing about Timmerman for some time. I probably should tell you that I haven't . . . involved myself in anything controversial for some time now. About eight years. So I was not investigating Timmerman. Not at all. And yet, some of my sources had kept contact with me. And they were telling me of incidents, primarily at Timmerman's rallies. People's rational consciousnesses permanently vacating their bodies. People hospitalized for sexual obsessions with inanimate objects. Marriages broken up by sexual acts later deemed intolerable. In Boston six months ago, three teenage girls left the rally, went to a nearby mall and cut up some poor man buying an anniversary present – a nightgown – for his wife.'

I leaned back. I could feel a tingling along my arms and legs. 'Why has none of this got into the papers?'

'Good question. When I first heard the stories I wondered about that, but frankly, I didn't really care. Since Jack died, I've been thinking about that a great deal.'

I thought, I'll bet you have. I remembered all the days and nights I'd spent thinking of nothing but Paul, and how those snakes could have gotten to him when the SDA had promised to protect him.

Alison was saying, 'I began to investigate.' She smiled. 'Despite my eight-year hiatus, some habits are hard to break. I began with that question. I spoke to people from the papers, the networks. Some of the incidents they knew about, some they'd never even heard of. In each case, however, a decision was made somewhere along the line to suppress the story. Often, it seems, without any conscious connection to the previous cases. Mary Howell, at the *LA Times*, seemed genuinely surprised and upset when I pointed out to her that she had decided against Timmerman stories on three separate occasions. I suggested to her that she print the story now. "Emerging pattern, disturbing questions." She promised me she would think about it. Think about it? Of course, nothing has been printed.'

'Do you think she was being straight with you? Maybe the government is clamping a lid on it.'

'Of course I thought about that. But I couldn't find any trace of government interference. And why would the government want to protect Alexander Timmerman? He certainly doesn't represent business as usual, which is generally the government's first priority.'

I said, 'The rally today didn't have anything like riots, or orgies.'

'No, no, it doesn't happen every time. Still, you must have noticed the intense sexual energy among the people who were blessed.'

I nodded, closing my eyes. I leaned back and thought about all the people touching each other, touching the trees, park benches, stones, anything they could get their bodies against. Alison said, 'It wasn't like that at the beginning. I've looked at TV footage of the early rallies. The people who received the blessing most often just stood there and cried. At the most, they would hug each other. Somewhere it changed.'

I said, 'Timmerman has Devoted Ones working for him. Could they be acting directly on the news media?'

'Possibly. And possibly it's a combination. When I started digging deeper, I caught the scent of some sort of government involvement, just not in the manner of actual censorship.'

'There was someone else at the rally,' I said. 'When the Beings were reaching out to bless the audience and everyone was hopping up and down, there was this woman at the back. Small, dressed all in black, with black hair. She didn't join the show but there was something about her. One moment she was just there, and then a little later she was gone.'

Alison shook her head very slightly and smiled. 'Her name,' she said, 'is Margaret Light-at-the-end-of-the-Tunnel 23. She appeared out of the Living World in August of last year and immediately reported with the Spiritual Development Agency as a companion-protector for Alexander Timmerman.'

I was trying to remember anything else about the woman – the Benign One, I should say – when someone called my name. I looked up and two of my friends, Kathy and Sharon, were coming towards me. 'Hi, gorgeous,' Sharon said in her chirpy voice, 'preparing for your life of leisure again?'

'Just grabbing it wherever I can get it,' I said. Reflexively I took off my glasses, then instantly regretted it. Just in time I stopped myself from jerking them back on again.

Kathy glanced at Alison, then looked past her at me and raised a plucked eyebrow. I said, 'Kathy Patterson, Sharon Cianetta, Alison Birkett.' To my surprise, I found myself wondering if I'd done that correctly, if you say the older person's name last or first. 'Alison's an old friend,' I said, and noticed Kathy's smirk on 'old'. Extremely tall – six feet three inches – Kathy grew up embarrassed and ashamed of sticking out above all the boys, let alone the girls, until one day she got a good haircut, put on some makeup and a short skirt, and discovered she was beautiful. Now she spends half her time looking in mirrors and the other half designing software for a cosmetics company – except when she's gossiping about her friends.

Kathy said, 'Guess who we saw together on 4th Street?' She paused, then announced, 'Jocelyn and Rebecca.'

'You're kidding,' I said. 'Does this mean they'll stop trying to divide all their friends for restaging the Revolution?'

'It means more than that, sugar,' Kathy said. She turned to Sharon. 'Do you want to tell her?'

In style, Sharon looks a little like a junior Kathy, though in fact she's a year older, a head shorter and a size plumper. She told me, 'They were standing in front of that jewellery store, you know, the one with the *wedding rings*, and holding hands and making noises like cute little animals.'

'My God,' I said, laughing. 'The tragic breakup of the ages founders on the rock of salvation. Do you think they'll send out announcements? Or maybe letters of apology for all the agony they've caused the rest of us.'

'Speaking of salvation and agony,' Kathy said, 'I happened to call Joan Monteil just a few short minutes ago.'

'Oh, did you now?' I said. 'And what did sweet little Joanie have to say for herself?'

'Oh, not much.' Kathy paused. 'She did have quite a lot to say about you, though.'

'Really,' I said. 'I may have to have a little chat myself with Ms Monteil.'

Kathy said, 'I think she wants to bring you into her kindergarten class for show and tell.' She patted my cheek. 'Cheer up, darling, at least she's cute.'

Sharon said, 'Maybe the two of you could double with Jocelyn and Rebecca.'

'Or we could all buy a house on Staten Island,' I said. 'Look, Sweetie, I'd love to have the two of you torment me all afternoon, but I have some things to discuss with Alison.'

After the two of them had exchanged 'Nice to meet you's' with Alison and wandered off to the smoking section, Alison sat back, looking at me like someone who's discovered an extra piece in a finished jigsaw puzzle. She said, 'Do you always remove your glasses when your friends come in?'

I shrugged. 'It helps with the image.'

'Image?'

'You know what they say. Girls don't make passes at girls who wear glasses. I believe that was proposition

23 from Adrienne Birth-of-Beauty's Shout From The
Skyscraper. If not, it should have been.'

'You could wear contact lenses,' she said, and I thought,
Great Mother Agony, is this why she tracked me down
after ten years? But then she raised an eyebrow and her
voice, in perfect imitation of Kathy, and said, 'That way
you could see who was making the passes. You could avoid
robbing the kindergarten.'

I felt oddly like an adolescent who's just discovered that
Mommy knows all those dirty words she and her friends
use to show how tough they are. I said, 'You still haven't
answered my question.'

'No, you're right. Why did I want to see you? I suppose
I wanted your take on Timmerman. I'm too close to it.
Because of Jack. And my investigators – well, they're good
at research, not analysis.'

'So you thought of me.'

She paused. 'Yes.'

'What do your sources say?'

'Very little. Just that Timmerman seems to have the
Living World on his side and no one wants to touch
him.'

'And the police?'

'I spoke with them after Jack died. They implied that
Jack had entered voluntarily into a perilous state, and
that since his death had resulted from contact with Benign
Ones, they must consider it beneficial. They gave it the
official verdict, "Death by ecstasy." '

'In other words,' I said, 'he died happy.'

'Exactly.'

'There's something,' I said, 'something just . . . wrong
about all this. I mean, besides the obvious. Something that
doesn't make sense.'

'I know. Ellen, if you're willing, I would like to have
you come to my office where I could show you my files.
Perhaps you might catch something I've missed.' She
added quickly, 'If you'd rather not, just say so.'

'I don't know,' I said. 'Maybe if you could give me a few days, let me think about it.'

'Yes, of course.' Suddenly she was looking down at her empty teacup. 'And Ellen . . . whatever you decide, it's good to see you again.'

'Yeah, well, thanks,' I said, then thought, come on El, give it a break. 'I better get back to work,' I said. 'Procrastination is its own reward, but it doesn't pay the rent.' I caught the waitress's eye.

'Shall I walk you back?' Alison said.

'Sure. I mean, thanks.'

In the street, it struck me that there was a time when nothing would have thrilled me more than walking side by side with Alison Birkett, having her consult me on an important case. To my surprise, I found myself wanting to cry. When we reached the lobby of my building, I told her, 'I'd invite you up for tea, but it's the sixth floor and the elevator's broken.'

'That's fine,' she said, just as a whirring noise signalled the arrival of the elevator from upstairs.

Though Alison pretended not to notice, I waved a hand and said, 'I lied. The fact is, I just don't like elevators.'

2

Absolutely not, I told myself. No way was I going to involve myself in some pet conspiracy project of Alison Birkett. So her friend got mashed by a mob. Maybe she could get him a gig as guardian of water coolers. She's good at that. If I did some checking, I told myself, it wasn't for *her*. I was just curious. I certainly wasn't going to go to her office and read any of her files. But what harm would it do, just for curiosity, to do some private enquiries into Great Brother Alex and his pet Devoted Ones? And besides, I needed to keep away from the house and the telephone. Now that she'd broken the ice (smashed it was more like it), Ms Birkett could take it into her head to call me at any moment. Or worse, Joan Monteil might call. I could screen my calls, but I hated jumping every time the phone rang, then waiting nervously through the next four rings and the outgoing message before whoever it was would come on the line.

So the next morning I set out for the library, where for three days I scanned through old magazines and newspapers for articles on Alexander Timmerman and his Consumer Liberation organization. I didn't expect any scandals or revelations. If Alison said none of the disturbing events had gotten into the newspapers I believed her. On that level I was sure she knew what she was doing. I just wanted a sense of what Timmerman was about, the kind of issues he was raising, what legal actions, if any, he'd taken against corporations or the government, what impact the Choir of Angels was having beyond raising the spiritual (read sexual) temperature at his rallies. And I wanted to see what articles had appeared on Timmerman's dark-haired Friend, whom I was already calling in my mind, 'Maggie Tunnel Light'.

About the last, not much. In fact, very little appeared on the Benign Ones at all. *Spiritweek* had an article in the 'US Sanctification' section on Consumer Liberation, reporting that a third Devoted One had joined the 'campaign to revitalize America' as Timmerman's press person put it. There was, of course, no picture of Maggie. I remember hearing once that someone had invented a computer-linked camera that could create an 'enhanced definition' image of a Bright Being. Supposedly, the SDA had slapped a restraining order on the inventor and the camera never got produced. The article did run a photo of Timmerman in his mask and grey suit, with surges of light behind him, a trick I knew I could duplicate on my computer any time I wanted. The text said precious little. Timmerman and his aides described their 'profound gratitude' that the Living World was supporting their campaign to 'fulfil the promise of the Revolution on all levels of society'. At the same time, they insisted that they had not sought out Margaret at all, but rather that she had approached them, appearing in their office, 'in a vapour of love', just after their yearly convention. According to the article, Ms Light would not 'interact' directly with the public – no blessings in other words – but would help the inner staff 'direct our spiritual resources to the massive tasks lying before us'.

As for the other two – Albert Comfort the Children 6 and Jeannette Benevolent Fire 31 – Timmerman had not exactly summoned them either, not in the formal sense of an operation to secure a Benign One for personal service. According to the official Consumer Liberation line, Timmerman had suffered some personal trauma or other (they were coy about just what had happened, which probably meant sexual rejection) and had set out on a pilgrimage to the ruins of the nuclear power plant along the Hudson River. Either from accident or from deliberately coating himself in hot ash, Alexander came close to death, only to be healed by the sudden manifestation of Albert and Jeannette, who removed his burns and gave him his 'true face' (the helmet mask) as a sign of service.

I wondered how much of this puff story to believe. As flattering as it was to Timmerman, it somehow rang true with my own sense of the Happy Twins (my term for them). There was something simple minded about them, as if, like so many Devoted Ones, they just wanted to help humanity lift itself from pain. In one of the articles, Timmerman's press manager hinted that Albert and Jeannette were really one entity who appeared in two forms because of humanity's 'expectations of gender'.

Very little appeared beyond these official accounts. *The Times* ran a feature on the Devoted Ones in Timmerman's campaign, and more broadly on the place of the Living World in contemporary society, 'two generations after the Revolution'. Like so many *Times* articles, it managed to sound deep without saying much of anything. *The Washington Post* and *The Miami Herald of Power* and a few other papers ran editorials. None of them said much of anything, though the *Post* warned of the need for humans to 'make the tough decisions in the clear light of day'.

More interesting to me was a sense of the campaign itself – what Timmerman was trying to achieve. I'm not sure what I expected to find, maybe a lot of high rhetoric without any content or follow-up. And maybe, considering what I'd seen and what Alison had told me, I expected sexual imagery to inflate his speeches. The fact is, Timmerman actually said very little about sex. His speeches, especially in recent weeks, were indeed spiced with 'liberating all levels, including the intimate teachings of the Spirit', and other elegances. But mostly he stayed with the issues that had launched him – consumer safety, corporate fraud, government protection of insurance companies and other industrial monopolies. To my further surprise, his cadres had shown themselves to be remarkably effective, winning a range of battles, either through the courts or through boycotts, organized letter writing, depossession enactments and other direct actions.

Timmerman had begun his career with a highly publicized attack on Sacred Motors, charging that the hood totem for their Nightleopard car failed to establish soul configurations for safe journeys. In fact, Timmerman demonstrated, the supposed guardian did nothing at all and might as well not have been there.

Timmerman's headdress made its first appearance during the Sacred Motors' campaign when he began doing daily protection enactments outside corporate headquarters, enactments which attracted more and more people as news reports surfaced of Nightleopard accidents on deserted roads in clear weather, or new cars breaking down or catching fire. Without his enactments, Timmerman claimed, the disasters would have been more frequent and worse. Nevertheless, SM managed to get a court order forcing him to stop. Refusing, Timmerman went to jail, but a higher court ruled that the mass enactments were a collection of 'individual spiritual events' rather than an organized ceremony, which meant that SM would have needed restraining orders against every single person holding up a placard, or burning flash powder on pictures of SM's CEO, or moving dummies in radio-controlled models of Nightleopard cars. Finally, the company gave up and released the records of the work done to draw up proper sanctification for the car before release to general sales. Two weeks later the car was withdrawn.

While none of Timmerman's later cases had attracted

that much publicity, his workers, known as 'the barefoot lawyers' for their fanaticism, had scored a run of large and small successes, taking on everything from soup companies to federal bureaucracies. As I skimmed the press reports, I noticed all the hard work behind Timmerman's rhetoric, the nuts and bolts and research and carefully built legal challenges that had made a registered sanctified letter from Consumer Liberation a terrifying sight for any executive or government official.

When the stories approached the present, say the past six months, something else emerged. I began to pick up a shift in emphasis from manufactured products and insurance companies to the banking system. There were charges and actions against specific banks, accusations of corruption, mismanagement, bad loans and even bribes, but more and more Timmerman had begun to attack the structure as a whole, claiming that the laws themselves undermined the national economy through leveraged buyouts financed by unregulated banks, manipulated stock investments using information about paper loans and 'a suicidal breakdown of the necessary barriers between the people who lend the money and the people who spend it'. There were rumours that Timmerman was planning to sue the Spiritual Development Agency for permission to lead an enactment in the Stock Exchange, by the body of Rebecca Rainbow, creator of the modern banking system in the chaos after the Revolution.

All this took me some three days to scrape together. I could have spent weeks reading everything, but I just wanted an outline, a silhouette, of Timmerman and his organization. My real target was still the Choir of Angels, and in particular my pet fascination, the Friend lurking in the background, Margaret 23. And about her, I could get no fix at all.

After three days, I found myself slouched in a library chair, my hands jammed into the pockets of my baggy jeans, as I growled at a stack of magazines. What was it about Tunnel Light? What was she doing there? Alison would know something, or at least have the resources for me to find out. I snarled once more at the magazines, and then began gathering them together to return them to their bins.

I headed home and booted up the computer. When I was learning to work graphics programs, I taught myself some other tricks as well. Ways of breaking into files, cracking codes, all that good stuff. For a while, it meant hanging around with some extremely obnoxious boys, but once I got the feel of it I could continue on my own. At the time, I told myself it was just something to do, a game, and besides, if some people could do such things, why shouldn't I be one of them? Now, watching the screen, I wondered just why investigatory skills had been so important to me.

I was about to try some routines, pick my way into a few locked boxes, when I suddenly stopped and stared at the screen. Don't be paranoid, I scolded myself. No one's watching you. And besides, you know how to stay anonymous, right? That *is* the point, isn't it? But I still turned off the machine.

Two hours later, I had checked into a hotel in midtown, the kind of place Mid-Westerners check into after saving up for their trip to the big city to see some skyscrapers and Broadway musicals. Claiming my cousin was going to join me, I rented two adjoining rooms with a connecting door. After paying cash up front, so I wouldn't have to use a credit card or my real name, I carried my suitcases up the stairs to the rooms and got to work. The rooms were lousy of course, no view other than the back of an office building and a loud banging from some nearby service room. Young single women have got to be the absolute bottom of the connector pole in the hotel managers' guide to life. Still, I was only planning to stay for a few minutes, so it hardly mattered. All that really counted was that the hotel was large enough that you could dial the rooms directly, without having to go through a human-operated switchboard.

I bowed to the room guardian, a cute little thing on a table between the two beds, and scattered some rock salt, fresh basil and cookie crumbs taken from my own house around the base of the husk, which took the form of a matronly woman holding a bowl. Asking for a blessing for privacy and selfless purpose, I poured some whisky into the bowl, then sucked it up with a straw and spat it out onto the floor. Then I got to work.

From my suitcases I took out one of the two computers and a pair of modems. I hooked up the computer and one of the modems to the telephone in the first room and then the second modem to the telephone in my 'cousin's' room, finally running some cheap telephone cable (bought in Radio Temple in the Village) between the two modems. I only had to tell myself about twenty times, 'Better paranoid than sorry.' Before leaving the rooms I set up a door switch with burglar tape, so that anyone opening either door would automatically shut off both phone lines.

Carrying my second suitcase, a carryon bag, I got a room in a hotel a few blocks away. There I unpacked the other computer and the last modem. When I'd connected them to the phone I was finally ready to start. I called the first hotel room, the one with the computer, and used that phone to call room 2. With room 2 as the number of record I called a value-added network, one of those companies which channels your local call into long-distance modem connections. And through *that*, I made my first real call to the offices of Consumer Liberation.

Back when I was getting past the lower levels of hacking I had the great fortune to pick up a woman one night who knew one of the masters, Annie-O, a genuine cross-gendered computer outlaw. I'm not sure what it is about computers and gender people, maybe something to do with changing realities. But it's certainly true that people like Annie can slide into locked programs the same way they slide from one gender to another. There was something else about Annie-O that made it unforgettable to meet her. She was an enactment master, a woman of power, having led her sisters across gender and spirit barriers over many years. Annie let me apprentice myself to her, and though we both knew I would never really find my way in the virtual worlds ('It's your clinging to a fixed gender,' Annie would tell me), I did learn enough for operations like breaking into Consumer Liberation.

Basically, I set up a dummy program which imitated their own, so that someone who tried to hook into them would get me asking 'Password, please?' and think it was them. Mr Legitimate Caller dutifully typed in the password, at which point I hung up. This brought him back to the real program, asking 'Password, please?' He no doubt assumed he'd typed wrong the first time, entered the password and thought no more of it. Only now, I knew the magic words as well. Thanks, Annie.

Only – there wasn't all that much to learn breaking into CL. Oh, if I'd been some insurance flunky I might have checked out their secret plans for enactments against malpractice fraud. Or I might have run up lists of planned rallies and other trivia. But as for secret goals and agendas, there just didn't seem to be any. Consumer Liberation in private wasn't all that different than their public image.

The Devoted Ones did not seem to figure much in the daily running of the organization. Everyone appeared grateful for the recognition bestowed on them by the Living World, not least because it impressed the public and drew people to their rallies. But the people who ran the organization, 'Timmerman's Tigers', as *Spiritweek* called them, were all lawyers and cared more about investigations and legal actions than mass blessings.

Maggie Tunnel Light hardly existed in CL's files. In my quick search I found only seven references to her, none of them of any significance. What was she doing there? She didn't work with the Tigers. She appeared to work directly with Timmerman. But how? Why was she there?

I did confirm one of my intutions. I ran a check on the number of files for particular issues. In the past year, more and more resources had gone into one subject – banking. One of Timmerman's chief lawyer hot shots, Samuel Jervis, appeared almost obsessed by what he called in a memo 'the deep structural rot in the edifice of American banking'. While the subject had only crept into Timmerman's speeches, the Tigers were pursuing it ferociously, gathering and analyzing masses of information, setting up task forces – bank failures, massive loan defaults, overnight millionaires, government coziness with bank directors and corporate raiders. It wasn't possible even to begin following it all, other than to get a sense of how maddening it was for the Tigers. Jervis's most recent memos talked of needing a 'focus', some particular revelation that could get people's attention long enough to make them see what was happening.

Feeling dissatisfied, I backed out of Consumer Liberation's database. Now for the big guys, I thought. Time to break into the SDA.

The Spiritual Development Agency was of a totally different order than Consumer Liberation. No cute dummy program was going to get me SDA passwords. However, I had something better. A phone number. Annie-O and her people considered what they did to be a sacred obligation, opening tunnels between the virtual world and the physical. For Annie, secrets threatened the flow of spirit energy between the worlds, and so they dedicated themselves to cracking open the walls as soon as the government tried to seal them up again. It wasn't enough just to break the secrets, they had to share them. They couldn't publish them, but they could make them available to anyone whom they'd invited into their network. I'm not sure what it was that Annie saw in me, a fixed gender person after all, but when she gave me the phone number for 'the list' it was all I could do to keep from crying. I knew the kind of trust it meant.

I left the hotel and went to a diner with a pay phone in the back by the toilets. It had been two years since I'd tried the number. Now, holding the horn in one hand and a quarter in the other, I found myself scared that the number I had was no longer any good, that I'd come to a dead end, and scared most of all that it meant so much to me. I wasn't just doing it for myself, I knew. I wanted to impress Alison. I wanted to march into her office with some answers, tell her to go to hell, and then march out again. And something else. The more I looked at this Timmerman thing, at what was happening at his rallies, at this Margaret 23 who didn't seem to be doing anything, the more I just knew that there was something wrong here. Something that needed to reach the light. I jammed the quarter in and punched the number.

A computer voice told me, 'Please state the name of the organization and sub-branch, if applicable. You have seven seconds.'

'Spiritual Development Agency', I said. 'Registration and function of Benign Ones to specific parties.'

There was a pause and then the voice came back with a five-word phrase. A moment later, the line went dead. A small smile grew to half my face as I put the phone back on the hook. 'All right, you bastards,' I whispered. 'I'm going to get inside you.'

Back to the hotel room. More nerves as I got my lines running again and moved my way into the SDA. As I took a breath before using the pass phrase, I sprinkled the keyboard and monitor with a few extra grains of my personal mix of spirit powder, given to me by my parents' Teller on my inner ecology name day after my first period. I typed in the phrase and a moment later the screen came alive with instructions, and I knew the files lay open for me.

I started with the Happy Twins, Albert and Jeannette,

just as a check. I didn't learn anything new, though I have to say I wasn't expecting to. It was Maggie Tunnel Light I was really after. First I verified the few facts I knew, her appearance last year, her immediate registration as a Benign Agent for – and this surprised me slightly – not Consumer Liberation, as the Twins had done, but Alexander Timmerman. Timmerman, I thought. Why Timmerman personally?

I went on to explore just what it was Margaret 23 did for Timmerman. And here the SDA files didn't seem to help any more than the newspapers. 'Advice.' 'Support.' 'Encouragement.' What did that mean? What did she *do*? And why didn't her file *say* what she did?

Okay, I thought. She's Timmerman's personal agent. Let's go back to the beginning of his connection. I asked the SDA computer to give me an account of the Summoning, when Timmerman drew her out of the Living World to do whatever it was she did for him.

I stared at the screen. 'No reference.' In some way, I was phrasing the question wrong. But why? It seemed straightforward enough. I decided to backtrack, start with the basics again. I asked it when Timmerman summoned her. 'No reference.' I shook my head. The damn machine just gave me the date, only a few minutes before. I began to wonder if some Malignant virus had invaded the SDA systems. A nice idea, I decided, but couldn't it have waited until after I got what I needed? But no, Malignant Ones in a system usually filled the screen with gibberish. I was just asking the wrong questions.

I slapped the table. Maybe Timmerman hadn't summoned her. Maybe she'd arrived spontaneously, with an urgent need to attach herself to Timmerman. Usually, I thought, free agent Beings didn't belong to any particular human or cause, but I was hardly an expert. So I asked the computer if Tunnel Light had entered our world on her own. No.

I said out loud, 'Well then, *someone* must have summoned her.' And then I laughed. Of course. It didn't have to be Timmerman himself. It could have been one of the Tigers, maybe an enactment specialist. I typed in, 'Who summoned Margaret Light-At-The-End-Of-The-Tunnel 23?'

The screen told me, 'Carolyn Park-Wu.' I sat back and made a face. From all the reading I'd done, I was pretty sure I knew the names of all of Timmerman's inner circle. Who was Carolyn Park-Wu? Some cousin or sister-in-law? I asked about her relationship to Timmerman. No reference. Great, I thought. Terrific. Someone with no relationship to Timmerman summons a Bright Being to act as his personal agent, for no particular purpose.

Feeling giddy, I asked what purpose Park-Wu stated when she registered the Summoning. The giddiness left immediately and I found myself shaking. 'National Security Sanctification,' the screen read, and for the first time I realized that this was serious, this was not a game. The SDA was the organization which issued security sanctifications. And now they were slapping one on their own files?

Leaving the machine on – I didn't want to take a chance on losing the contact – I went down to the hotel lobby and called Alison's office. 'This is Ellen Pierson,' I said in my best no-nonsense voice. 'I need to speak to Ms Birkett, immediately.'

She came on right away, with a catch in her voice as she said, 'Ellen? Hello. I'm glad you called.' Somewhere it struck me that she'd been afraid she wouldn't hear from me, and I wondered what exactly that meant. But I had no time to think about it.

'Alison,' I said, 'is this still a protected line?'

There was a pause, and then she said, 'Yes. Registered with the government—'

'I don't care about that. Do you know it's safe?'

'I was about to say that it's swept daily, by the best in the business.'

'Okay,' I said, 'then I need you to check on a name for me.'

'Sure,' she told me. 'Let me get a pen. Okay. Go ahead.'

'The name is Carolyn Park-Wu.'

In the brief silence, I felt like I could see her mind starting to click. She said, 'I don't need to check. I can tell you right now. Carolyn Park-Wu is a senior staff aide for Arthur Channing.'

The shaking was back. I said, '*Senator* Arthur Channing?'

'That's right.'

'Head of the Senate Finance Committee?'

'Yes. Ellen, what have you found?'

To myself, I whispered, 'Holy shit.' Out loud I only said, 'Alison, we need to talk. Can we meet somewhere?' She suggested a hotel by Glowwood Sanctuary, the private park off 19th Street. When we hung up, I stood for a moment by the telephone, my hand still holding on to the receiver. Why did I do that, I thought. Why? I didn't want to see her. I didn't want to get involved in her damned schemes. This was serious. This was the SDA and now the Senate. I thought, maybe I should call her back.

Instead, I went up to the room and sat staring at the screen. Shut it down, I told myself. Get out, now. Instead, I typed another question. Alison has since said that this question marks what she calls my special talent. When I told her I had no idea what made me ask it, what, if anything, I was looking for, she just laughed and said that that was the point. The question was, 'Has the Bright Being Margaret Light-At-The-End-Of-The-Tunnel 23 ever appeared in any other configurations?'

'National Security Sanctification' came the answer, and this time the shaking was uncontrollable.

3

Before going to see Alison, I washed my hair and changed to a pair of tight black jeans and an oversized white shirt I'd bought on sale the day before. Ridiculous, I told myself as I cut a small hole in the shirt, below the spare button, for the Living World to infuse the fabric. Why was I still trying to impress her? I didn't even like her. It reminded me of when I was in high school and used to visit my Aunt Sylvia. I could never stand Sylvia, her big word condescension towards my mother, her pleated blouse and proper black pumps, her comments that I 'really could look very nice' if I 'just made a serious effort'. And yet, every time I went to see her I would try to *show* her, even if negatively, by wearing or saying something outrageous. It's just like Aunt Sylvia, I told myself, putting on eyeliner and lipstick. Sure. Right.

When I arrived at the hotel bar, Alison was already there, sitting upright in a red leather chair by a small round table to the side of the polished bar. She smiled as she waved me over. She was wearing a dark blue blazer and skirt, a soft cream–coloured shirt with large black buttons and flat open-toed black sandals. She had a chunky silver bracelet on her right wrist and a plain watch with a black leather strap on the left. She'd clipped her hair back on the sides, showing off small web-like earrings set with clusters of tiny blue stones. Like me, she was wearing lipstick and subtle eye makeup (except my eyes were not so subtle). I don't think I'd ever seen her looking so fem before. Or so pretty.

'I'm afraid you're seeing me in my court incarnation,' she said. 'I feel like some comic-book character. Trial Lady.'

'I hope you charmed the judge,' I said.

She took a sip of her drink. 'I imagine I did. I won.' She looked up at me and grinned.

She was drinking whisky with ice, which is usually my drink when I want to get serious. When the waiter came, I ordered a pina colada, a drink I usually can't stand. 'How is your friend Harry?' Alison asked me.

'I haven't seen him since the rally.' To myself, I thought I would be damned if I was going to make small talk with her.

'I liked him,' she said. 'He seemed like someone who knows how to think.'

'I'll tell him you said that.'

Finally the waiter came and set down my absurd frothy drink. I took a sip and made a face. For a moment I thought Alison was grinning at me, but when I looked she was leaning forward with her hands clasped. 'You've been doing some digging,' she said.

I took a deep breath. 'Timmerman is being set up. Margaret Tunnel Light –' She didn't react to the condensed name. '– is a plant.' I paused, but she said nothing. So I told her about Consumer Liberation's exploration of banking and the fact that MTL came from Park-Wu. 'Obviously, there's a lot that's still unexplained, but I'm convinced that Great Brother Alex's new Friend is not there to help him.'

'Are you saying she's Malignant and not Benign?'

'No,' I said. 'I don't think so. If the SDA calls her Benign, I think we have to trust that designation. These were their own files, not for general publication.'

Alison sat up straight and closed her eyes. One finger pressed her lips, as if she was telling herself not to speak.

I thought I knew what she was going to say and I was readying myself to tell her it was none of her business how I got my information. Instead, when she opened her eyes, she said, 'She could just be a spy. A means of checking up on what Timmerman is doing. So Channing wouldn't be made to look foolish by some sudden revelations.'

'Possibly. Only, couldn't they just infiltrate some human into the organization? It just seems to me a Benign One as a spy would be hard to control.'

Alison said, 'That would hold as well for some sort of plot against Timmerman. More so, since Channing would be asking the Being to act against its client.'

'Its official client. It could be working entirely for Channing. Or Park-Wu.'

'The problem,' Alison said, 'is still persuading a Devoted One to act in a duplicitous manner. I don't claim to be an expert in this field, I'm afraid I've spent more time dealing with Ferocious Ones, but from what I know of Benign Ones, having to act as an enemy, or a spy for that matter, would seem to set up a very painful contradiction.'

'Even if Channing convinced Tunnel Light that Timmerman was evil in some way? And that it would be serving humanity by helping to destroy him?'

Alison sat back and took a sip of her drink. I thought I noticed her glance at my untouched colada and had to fight an impulse to force some down. She said, 'It all comes back to Tunnel Light's function. Which, as you point out, the SDA files seem to avoid delineating. Why is she there? What is she doing?' I said nothing. 'And there's still the question of the . . . outbreaks at Timmerman's rallies. What connection could they possibly have with banking?'

'Alison—' I said. She stopped talking. 'Look, I dug into this stuff, because, because it interested me. I was just curious to see what I could find out. But I'm not going to continue. I've got my own things to do, okay?'

Alison said, 'Oh. Oh, I'm sorry, Ellen. I didn't mean to

presume anything. I suppose I just got excited. I realize it's my issue.'

I stood up. 'It's probably best if I just go.'

Looking up at me, she seemed suddenly sad, or maybe frightened. I discovered a desire to reach out and stroke her cheek. She said, 'Yes, of course. Thank you, Ellen. Thank you for your help.' I picked up the blue and grey knapsack I use for a purse. 'Ellen?' Alison said. I looked at her. 'I'm sorry if I've offended you in some way. That was not my intention.'

'I'm sure it wasn't,' I said. As I left, I thought to myself, why do I have to be so hard on her? And then, why am I feeling like some goddamn villain?

When I got home I began to clear my desk of all the letters and other junk that had accumulated over the past three days while I was playing investigator. Several times I thought of calling Harry to see if his sharp eye could help me make sense of what was happening. I even rehearsed starting the conversation, something like 'You've got an admirer. Remember that friend of mine we met in Miracle Park?' But I didn't want to tell him about my electronic b and e, or about Timmerman, let alone how I first came to know Ms Birkett. So I decided instead I should just get to work.

I might have dropped the whole thing if not for a visit from the federal government. They were waiting for me in my apartment two days later when I came home from the art supply store on 3rd Avenue. Three of them, two men and a woman. They must have heard me opening the door and stayed silent, because I had no idea anyone was there, until I came round the hallway into my living room/workroom. When I came in, they stood, very politely, as if their mothers had trained them in etiquette, which I suppose was the case, since fed agents supposedly speak of the agency as Mother Truth, and hold fire and mud enactments to bond to Her for life.

Of course, I tried to run as soon as I saw them. This was New York, after all. But one of them, the woman, held up her badge and told me, 'It's all right, Ms Pierson. SBI. We just want to talk with you.' Goddamnit, I thought, why can't they be thieves?

They reminded me a little of the SDA operatives back when I was a kid. They were wearing masks, though not of animals. These were cylindrical, smooth, with faces painted on a surface that looked like old-fashioned printed circuits. Little lights set into the plastic (I assumed it was plastic) flickered on and off in patterns either random or beyond my ability to follow. But then, I wasn't in much of a mood for concentrating. Instead of the SDA's overalls, they wore clothes my Aunt Sylvia might have approved of – brown suits for the men, a knee-length long-sleeved dress with buttons down the front for the woman. Instead of paintings at the crotch, their clothes held mirrors, both there and on their shoes. On the right side of the neck, and on their wrists disappearing up their arms, I could see enactment scars, jagged lines alternating in different directions. Just under the left ear was a brand, something that looked like a simplified version of the badge the woman had shown me. I'm not sure what spiritual bonding the brands and scars served, but they did make it easier to believe these guys were really agents; an imposter would have to be a real perfectionist to bodyalter just for a stunt.

'Why don't we all sit down?' the woman said. Keeping my eyes on her, I sat on the canvas director's chair Harry had given me for my birthday.

Speaking in a high nasal voice that made me wonder if he might be a drag king, one of the men told me, 'We've come here, Ms Pierson, as a kind of favour.' How nice, I thought. 'Your government is concerned that you seem to be involving yourself in matters that really have nothing to do with you. And which could lead to very serious consequences.' I said nothing.

After a moment, the other man said, 'We're sure you realize, Ms Pierson, that tapping into government files is a federal offence, punishable by up to twenty-five years in prison.'

Goddamnit, I thought, so much for playing motels and modems. But then it struck me – if they really had caught me, if they had any evidence, why weren't they taking me away? So maybe they were drawing some conclusions. But how? Alison, I thought. They've got people following her, recording her conversations. I wondered if we would have been safer in her office.

On cue, the first man said, 'Your government is concerned about your involvement with Ms Alison Birkett.'

They seemed to expect me to say something, so I put in, 'I'm not involved with her. She's just someone I know. I saw her recently for the first time in, I don't know, ten years.'

The woman said, 'Then perhaps a break of another ten years would be a wise idea.'

The second man said, 'As you will remember, Ms Pierson, your previous involvement with Ms Birkett did not end happily.'

I thought, you sonofabitch, Alison didn't kill Paul, *you* did. You and your pet Malignant Ones. You and your goddamn cover-ups.

The first man put in, 'Your government would not like to see another tragedy. It would make sense, Ms Pierson, to keep away from Ms Birkett.'

I said, 'Well, I wasn't planning to see her again.'

They stood up, so I did too. The woman said, 'And please. No more tricks with off-limits information.' When I said nothing they left.

Alone again, I sank down in a chair, only to bolt up and grab the flash powder and some feathers and rock salt from the altar in the bedroom. Opening the door, I scattered the salt all about the threshold, outside and in, and then on the floor around the chairs they'd been sitting in. I sprinkled the flash powder over the salt and set it off, waving the feathers in large sweeps through the air and calling out 'Seal all openings of this house my body from anger and pollution, from the one who whispers and the one who screams, from the one who hammers and the one who cuts, from all enemies and liars and unnatural death. Yes!'

When I'd finished and sat down again, I discovered I was crying. For some reason I thought of those bastards calling Alison 'Ms Birkett' and I promised myself I would never think of her that way again.

What was I going to do? Should I warn her? How? If I called her, or went to see her, or even mailed her a letter, they could find out about it. I could send one of those paste-up jobs, with words cut out from the newspaper. Or maybe I could follow her from a distance, and when she went to a Chinese restaurant bribe the waiter to slip a warning into the fortune cookie for the ceremony at the end of the meal. I laughed. Something Annie-O once said to me came into my mind. 'You've got to remember, Ellen, this is the end of secrets. Anyone can find out anything. If you've got something to hide, learn to hide in front of things instead of behind them.'

I stood up and grabbed my knapsack purse. As I was heading downstairs a thought came into my mind, a replay. 'Alison didn't kill Paul. The government did.'

I ended up walking to her office, getting madder and madder as I pumped my way through the streets, until when I got to her building I burst in the door and strode up to the doorman and demanded, 'Where's the stairs?' It took a phone call to 'Ms Birkett' (I wanted to shout at him not to call her that) to get him to unlock the door to the stairwell.

Alison was at the door to her office when I made it to the tenth floor (stopping on the eighth to catch my breath). 'Ellen,' she said, 'what is it? Are you okay?'

'I'm not sure,' I said. 'Let's go inside.' Briefly, I thought of going somewhere else to avoid any ears in the walls, but at least this place was swept. Daily, she said. That hotel certainly hadn't protected us. Thinking of Annie-O's advice, I sat down in the leather chair alongside the desk. 'I've had a visit,' I said.

When I had told her what had happened, she bent her head forward and rested it in her hands. When she lifted it again, she looked scared. 'Ellen . . .' she said, and stopped. She took a deep breath. 'I've gotten you into something I never should have gotten you into. Damnit, I should have just left you alone.'

'It sounds like they're after you much more than me.'

'That doesn't matter. I can protect myself. Connections, remember?'

I'm not sure why I was being so reasonable, why I wasn't more scared, but I said, 'Well, then, extend them to me.'

'Yes, of course,' Alison said. 'I already have. At one level, I'm sure they just wanted to scare you. The fact is, Ellen, they can't actually touch you without buying themselves more trouble than it's worth. Especially when they'd just be doing someone else's dirty work.'

'Great,' I said. 'Then why are you worried?'

'The government . . . the government is not the point. Ellen, look, I've got to confess something. I didn't just look you up to get your opinion. I . . . I wanted to see you. To see what you were like. See who you'd become. I'm afraid I used this Timmerman investigation as an excuse, and I guess a hook, to get involved with you. And to get you involved with me. Damnit.'

'I don't understand,' I said, and knew I was lying. 'Why did you want to get involved with me?'

'You had . . . you stayed in my mind. As the time went by, I found myself thinking about you. Not all the time. Every now and then, at odd moments, something would just make me think of you. And I'd think how much time had passed.'

Softly, I said, 'How I wasn't a child any more?'

'Yes.' She said nothing for a moment, only looked at me. Some of the strength had come back into her face. She said, 'And then the thing with Timmerman happened. With Jack.'

'And that gave you your golden opportunity.'

Instead of getting angry, she shook her head slightly and smiled. 'I guess that's true, in a way. Not deliberately, God knows. Jack was killed and I was devastated. And furious. Once again, someone, it's still not clear to me who, was chewing up people's lives, hurting and killing people close to me.'

'Which naturally led you to think of me.'

She took a breath. 'Naturally, or not, I certainly thought of you. I couldn't get you out of my mind. Ellen, it was all mixed up. I wanted to see you, I wanted your help, I wanted to know—'

'How I'd turned out?' She nodded. 'How your experiment in hero worship had developed.'

'I never asked you to worship me. I never even asked to be your hero. If anyone was experimenting, it was you.'

'I was a kid, Alison. Kids are supposed to experiment.'

'God, don't you think I know that?'

There was a pause, and then I said, 'And now you found yourself thinking of me.'

'Yes.'

'And you wanted me back in your life?'

'Yes.'

I said, 'So that's how it works. Set them up when they're young, then come back and harvest them ten years later.'

'Your family came to me, Ellen. I didn't spot you and put some sort of claws into you. I never treated you as some sort of prey.'

'But you didn't discourage me, either.' She looked

down and shook her head. 'You let me hang around like a puppydog, thinking you were the greatest thing since the Revolution.'

'I'm sorry, Ellen. You're right. I should have been more conscious.'

'Don't you think you should find a better means to do these things? I mean, first my cousin gets killed and now your friend. The next time you want to set up some little girl, then come back for her thirteen years later, maybe you can do it without anybody getting murdered.'

Her eyes narrowed and her hands clenched, and for a second I really thought she was going to hit me. When she spoke, however, she only said, 'Do you really believe that that's what happened, Ellen? That I just saw that mess with the SDA as an excuse to go after a little girl? I cared about you because you were special, Ellen. When I found myself thinking about you these past months, don't you think I asked myself the same questions you're asking now? Don't you think I looked at what I was doing, what I had done back then? I did my best then, Ellen. I tried as hard as I knew how to help you and your family. I failed. I'm sorry. There's nothing else I can do about it.'

'Maybe if you hadn't put so much energy into giving me little compliments and having me come panting round your desk—'

'No. I won't accept that. I did my absolute best on that case. I put all my energy into it. And while I liked seeing you, I didn't make some special effort to lure you into my world. You wanted to enter it. Should I have barred the way? Should I have refused to treat you as a friend?'

'Damnit,' I said, 'I was only fourteen.'

'Don't you think I knew that?'

'You knew fucking everything. Except how to save Paul.'

'Is it really Paul you care about, Ellen? Is that why you hate me? Or was it just that I turned out not to be perfect?'

It wasn't Alison who killed Paul. It was the government.
I shook my head, flinging away the thought. I said, 'That
must have been as big a surprise to you as it was to
me. God, Alison, you were the most conceited person
I'd ever met.'

She looked surprised for a moment, then burst out
laughing. 'And you're still the smartest. Is it so surprising
that I wanted to see you again?'

No, I thought. I'm not getting caught up in this. 'Good,'
I said. 'So you've seen me. And so has the government.'

She sighed. 'Yes. Ellen . . . I'll . . . I'll let them know
that you're out of it. That you have nothing to do with
any of this. I'll tell them how I pulled you in. And . . .
that I'm withdrawing from any investigations.'

'Sure,' I said. 'You got what you were after, didn't
you? You got to see me. Congratulations. So what if
your friend's dead or Timmerman's being set up? The
hell with them. You got me to come up to your office,
that's all that really matters.'

She didn't answer. 'Look,' I said, 'I'm going. I came
to warn you and I've done that, so great. If ten years
from now you can't resist seeing me, maybe you can
call me on the phone? Not wait for some Bright Being
to kill somebody?' Before she could challenge me, I made
my grand exit, marching out without bothering to close
the door.

Over the next few days I did my best to get back to
work, to seeing my friends. I made a date with Joan
– 'a nice uncomplicated lay' I promised myself – went
to a film festival with Harry and Glorybe, assured my
parents I'd come home for my cousin's daughter's Eighth
Day piercing enactment, had lunch with a neighbourhood
Teller who wanted me to design a poster for a Rising of
the Light street festival, and on and on. Whenever I found
myself thinking of Alison I made sure to growl and say out
loud, 'Goddamn bitch'. If I woke up in the middle of the

night thinking of her I just put on the radio or else got up and chanted the names of the Founders.

My government gave no signs of any further interest in me.

Four nights after my meeting with Alison, Alexander Timmerman came on a talk show. Though I told myself it was the last thing I needed to see, I found myself in front of the TV at 5 o'clock, instead of my drawing board. Timmerman looked relaxed, sitting there with his mask alongside him on the couch, talking about his work, about the gratitude and humility he felt that the powers of the Living World had chosen to bless him and his followers with their Gifts. I listened with my fist clenched, telling the screen, 'You jerk. You don't know what you're doing. They're setting you up. Don't worry about the twins, it's Tunnel Light who really counts. You idiot.'

When the show ended, I sat staring at the commercials as a fragment of my shouting match with Alison ran through my mind. 'Jack was killed,' Alison had said, and, 'Once again someone was chewing up people's lives.' I closed my eyes, took a deep breath, another. On the TV, the news had come on with some cheerful young man telling us all about somebody's vision in a city council meeting and how it had led to the mayor announcing a pilgrimage to the Forbidden Beach on Long Island. I used the announcer's voice as an alpha prayer machine, draining all the content from the sounds to let them smooth out my brain waves. Someone was chewing up people's lives. Paul and Jack and Alison and I thrown together. She didn't just use this as an excuse. There was a power in this. Bringing us together. Paul and Jack.

I made a noise and opened my eyes. 'Shit,' I said. Instead of an answer, another image had come into my mind. The computer screen just before I'd switched it off in that motel. The answer of 'National Security Sanctification' when I'd asked about any previous configurations for Margaret Light-at-the-End-of-the-Tunnel 23. I grabbed the phone, then put it down. Ridiculous, I told myself. If they're tapping anybody they're tapping her, protected line or not. But I still went out into the street for a pay phone. Illusions of comfort.

She answered the phone herself. 'It's me,' I said. 'I'm not calling to get back into anything, but I wanted to let you know about something I forgot to tell you. When I was doing my own checking.' Trying not to admit to any tampering I managed to let her know what had happened. 'I don't know what it means,' I said, 'but it's stayed in my mind. So I'm giving it to you to get it out of me. Okay?' She thanked me, managed to convey for whoever was listening that I wasn't involved and then we hung up. For a moment I stood there with my hand on the phone, until I noticed a woman behind me shifting her weight from one side to another as she made faces at the air. I sighed and went home.

The following night was my date with Joan. As the evening approached, I found myself wishing I could just order in some pizza and keep working. Instead, I told myself it was good for me to see her (I thought of my mother saying, 'You should get involved with people your own age' and answered her 'Joan Monteil and I will never be the same age as long as we live.') and made myself wash my hair and put on fresh jeans and a black cowgirl shirt with pearl buttonsnaps. And of course I left my glasses off. We all need to keep up our personal traditions.

Joan came in bubbling about a dream she'd had in which the two of us had gone down in separate submarines on some government mission to locate a Stone of Becoming for the president to give to the Emperor of Japan. As soon as she'd woken up, Joan had rushed to the Canal Street branch of the National Oneiric Registration Agency to run the dream through their computers. She showed me the printout. According to NORA, dreams of 'psychic and/or transformational artifacts or natural objects given or received as gifts' correlated with a high percentage ot submitted dreams for the previous three-day period from people who described themselves as 'establishing or deepening a profound interpersonal relationship'.

I changed the subject to where we would go for dinner. It wasn't just that I'd never dreamed of Joan, nor even that I could hardly imagine myself doing so. What really made me feel like a creep was the fact that Joan couldn't see that I just didn't feel about her the way she felt about me. She made it so easy to use her it became really difficult.

I did my best, though. I went out with her for curry, smiling and saying 'uh huh' while she told me about problems with her mother, putting her off as gently as I could when she suggested we go back to the Speaker for an update on the inner truth of our relationship. After an evening of this, I considered that I had earned a good workout in bed.

Joan had a way of completely surrendering her body to me, offering herself up as if I was her spirit guide and could draw entry gates all over her body for the Living World to fill her with light. Her openness to me was what I liked best about her, at least sexually – the way she would close her eyes and purr when I kissed her, or moan softly as I moved my tongue and fingertips slowly over her nipples, as if she would be happy for me to do just that for hours and hours, but then, when I would move my fingers down the middle of her body, from the forehead, over the closed eyes and the nose, feeling out the lips and the neck, moving sideways once more over the breasts, when I would move my hand like an animal on a warm mudslide, over the sweat of her vulva and into her lips, she would shriek in a way I never would have thought possible from her.

That night I was determined. I was going to make the evening a true landmark for the Revolution. I did pretty well, too, going through three surgical gloves and a good two feet of dental damming clingwrap. Joan did her part as well, surprising me with a gift from Sisters Under

The Skin, a women's sex shop near the 5th Avenue Teller's Hall. The gift was a two-part resonating guardian, something I'd seen but never tried. The rubber-sheathed penetrator was in the shape of a fish-tailed woman with arms folded over her breasts and long hair in waves all the way down her back. The resonator took the form of a bird-headed woman, standing with her chest pushed forward and her arms raised high in an arc. According to the instructions, circuitry in the penetrator picked up the energy of orgasm and broadcast it to its sister who then gave off a voice-like hum, modulating its pitch and volume as the quality of the orgasm changed.

I moved the penetrator into Joan without telling her so that she jumped at first, then settled back again, squirming into the mattress as if to get really comfortable, eyes closed, a happy smile on her face. Moving the fish woman in and out at different speeds or at different levels of force, I discovered I could change the bird song, creating weird melodies and even yelps, perfectly matching Joan's own ragged cries and shouts. Without realizing it I started singing along, crying out or humming as if there were resonators hidden in my brain and throat.

When Joan finished, however, when the bird woman finally stopped even her subliminal whispers, and Joan tried to start on me – I discovered I wasn't interested. I didn't want her hands in me, or her lips against my breasts, or any part of what she wanted to give me. I pushed her away as gently as I could, saying something like, 'I'm sorry, sweetie. I really liked making love to you, but it's kind of drained me.' She tried to joke about restoring me to life with her magic kiss, but I only turned away as she moved towards my mouth. 'Look,' I said, sitting up. 'I think I'm just worried about my work. It's not you. It's just really hard for me to let go when I'm stuck with a deadline.'

I did get some work done when Joan went home, as if to save my honour. But I really didn't care any more for work than I did for having Joan use me as a sounding device for bird-headed women. I kept thinking I should call Harry and ask him what I should do about Joan. Only, then I would have to tell him why I couldn't focus on her and that meant telling him about Alison, and worse, about Timmerman. So for the rest of the evening I found ways to procrastinate until it became time to go to sleep.

The next morning I was sitting on my black swivel chair in front of my drawing board, drinking green tea and feeling like now I really did need to get something done, when the doorbell rang. I thought, 'Shit, she's come back to tell me of some dream she's had and how NORA wants to invite us to Founders' City to meet the president.' But I knew it wasn't Joan. I could feel the other side of that door the way the bird lady could feel her fish sister's ecstasy. 'Hello, Alison,' I said as I opened the door.

She was wearing jeans and running shoes and a black warm-up jacket over a purple T-shirt. Her hair looked wild, as if she'd been running and hadn't had a chance to comb it, and she wasn't wearing any makeup or earrings. I realized I'd always seen her with earrings. Around her neck she wore a brass cylinder on a black silken cord. I guessed that the hollow cylinder contained a statement of spiritual intent along with tiny ceremonial relics of key points in her life and any blessed objects from her own visions and enactments. In other words, protection. 'May I come in?' she said. I nodded and stepped away from the door.

Alison stood facing me. I expected her to look around, perhaps to comment about how the room reflected who I was, or maybe concealed it. Instead, she just looked at me. I was about to remind her that she was the one who'd come to see me and maybe she could indicate why, when she said, 'It's her.'

My hand flattened against my own protection, still worn around my neck. 'I don't understand,' I said, though of course I did, I'd known all along, from the first moment seeing her standing there, behind Timmerman, watching the crowd while the Happy Twins blessed them into a frenzy. There was a power in this. Bringing us all together.

'Margaret Tunnel Light,' Alison said. '*She's Lisa Black Dust 7.*'

I think I started making some kind of noises, because Alison came towards me with her hands out, as if to comfort me. I jerked a hand up, like a traffic cop and she stopped immediately. With my other hand still pressed against my chest, I sat down on the chair by the drawing board. My breath wasn't working right, the in and out didn't seem in the normal order, but I managed to ask her, 'How did you find out?'

She pointed vaguely at the walls and I realized she couldn't say, it was illegal. More tampering. 'Sources,' she just said. 'I approached it from a different angle. The Tellers instead of the SDA.'

I nodded. Bending over, I did my best to take in a deep breath. When I straightened up, I said, 'They told us they would banish her. Send her back to the Living World. Goddamn bastards.'

Alison sat down on a wooden chair a few inches away from me. The closeness sent a kind of shock through me. She said, 'Technically, they did banish her. Reconfiguration requires that they break her down first. Technically, she's not the same.'

'Shit,' I said. 'Didn't I tell you Maggie was a goddamn Malignant One? Didn't I fucking say that?'

Alison sighed. 'I don't think so. I think they reconfigured her into a Benign One. I think that was the deal that allowed her to stay here in our world. That she break herself down and transform into benevolence.'

I shouted, 'Benevolence? Then what the hell is she doing there in Timmerman's organization? You *know* she's a plant.'

'Yes, I know,' Alison said. 'I still don't understand it.'

'Shit,' I said. I jerked the medallion from my neck

and threw it across the room. 'Shit! They're going to get Timmerman the way they got Paul. They're going to kill him, and it will all be for nothing, for some stupid fucking cover-up. And they'll give him some stupid pathetic appointment, guardian of bumper stickers or something. Oh, goddamnit.' I was crying. I couldn't decide if I should stop.

Alison leaned forward and put her arms around me. I nearly screamed at her, that it was all her fault, why couldn't she leave us all alone. But I didn't. Rolling my chair closer, I let her hold me, feeling safer than I'd ever felt with the SDA, while I cried into her neck. Later, I told Alison that the smartest thing she ever did was not to say anything at that moment. When I told her that, she grinned at me and said, 'I know.'

I cried for about thirty seconds and then started to pull away, but when Alison didn't let go I started to cry again. I thought of the last time she'd hugged me, after Paul's death. But I knew this was different.

Stopping finally, I dug a tissue from my pants and blew my nose. This time Alison loosened her hold and I sat up. I sat facing her, with my arms still draped around her back. I just kept looking at her, looking at the shape of her face, the placement of her eyes, her nose, her mouth like they were some sort of constellation, the texture of her face some kind of map. Then I bent forward, pulling her close again, and kissed her.

It didn't last long, but it had almost twenty years behind it. We separated, then hugged again, not at all like thirteen years ago, and then I took a chance and looked at her. It felt like a chance, as if she might look at me in some wrong way and ruin everything and I would have to hate her again. But she only sat very still, her arms around me, her face solemn, the eyes glistening as if she too might start to cry. I had the awful thought that she might apologize again, or tell me she didn't want to take advantage of me. When she spoke, however, it was only after her face changed to a smile. 'You took your glasses off,' she said.

I shrugged. 'They got all dirty from crying.'

She nodded. 'Can we go sit on the couch?' she said.

Holding her hand, I led her the few feet across the room. I kissed her again, without holding on too tightly, so that I could feel the gentle pressure of her breasts against mine. We kissed longer this time, still gently, not even using our tongues, and I thought it might be possible to melt into orgasm just from kissing.

But there was something else I had to take care of. I pulled away again and when I looked at her she was waiting for me, so that I knew I could say what had to be said. 'I want to go after them.'

She nodded. 'Yes. I know. You realize we might not get them? This is the government, after all.'

'I understand that. I just want to try. At least that.'

Alison said, 'This is hard for me, Ellen. I have to let go of feeling responsible for you. Feeling . . . feeling that I lured you into a trap.'

'Using yourself as bait?'

She ran her fingertips down the side of my face. 'I suppose so,' she said. 'Or maybe I used you as bait for yourself. And for me.'

I told her, 'This is a choice I'm making, Alison. I'm making it right now, without manipulation or coercion. I want to do this. If you refuse, I'll do whatever I can on my own.'

She shook her head. 'I don't refuse,' she said.

We started kissing again. I moved my fingertips down her back, between her shoulder-blades. When I reached the innermost part of the curve at the base of her spine I pressed sharply, and her body arched as she gasped. She looked at me in surprise and then began kissing me all over my face, very fast at first, then slowly, spending a long time moving her lips along my eyebrows and around the edges of my cheeks before finally returning to my mouth.

Once more, I pushed her away. 'There's something else,' I said. 'No deals. No letting them off the hook.'

She grunted, shook her head. 'Did anyone ever tell you,' she said, 'that you're one hell of a tough negotiator?'

I laughed. 'I mean it, Alison. No backroom arrangements.'

She took in a deep breath, let it out explosively. 'Give me a moment,' she said. She bent her head down with her eyes closed and pressed her hands against her thighs. At first I thought she was angry, but then I realized she was separating herself from me, making sure that the answer she gave didn't come from desire. I was wondering if I should put my glasses back on when she looked up. 'All right,' she said. 'No deals. Whatever we find we do our best to expose. You should know, Ellen, that we might not get very far. Arthur Channing is a serious man and there are even more serious men behind him.'

I said, 'I understand that.'

'I'm not entirely sure what we can do. To be honest, I'm not sure how long we'll last. I hope that I have enough dirt on enough people in enough safe places to keep us alive and out of prison. But if we make enough trouble we might just tip the balance against us.'

'At least we're going to try.'

'At least that.'

I said, 'And at least we're not hiding from each other.'

She smiled. 'I feel like we should recite the Blessing of the Saved.'

'Later,' I told her.

She held out her hands, palms up. I went past them, into her arms. If I'd had my glasses on, I would have tossed them away.

4

How do you start a love affair with someone you've been in love with for most of your life? How do you begin when you didn't even meet her for the first five years you loved her, when for another four you couldn't admit that such a feeling could live in you, and then for the next ten you tried to drive it out entirely? What do you say, what do you do, when you find out that *she's* in love with *you*? Do you forget all this history and pretend you've just met? Do you thank – someone (we couldn't thank the Benign Ones, not any more, so whom?) for twisting the world to grant your life's yearning? Do you wonder if she's tricked you, if she set this whole thing up, all those years ago? Do you wonder if you've set *her* up? If you don't know who to thank, who do you blame?

I realized, that first night Alison and I spent together, that I actually knew almost nothing about her. I could still run down a list of her most famous cases, at least the ones up until thirteen years ago. And I knew the shape of her face, the curl of her hair, the movement of her hands, her shoulders, her head as she spoke, the way she leaned forward when excited, or rocked back slightly when thinking, or especially calculating. But I didn't know about her growing up, or what she did when she was hanging out with her friends, or who those friends were, if she went to professional parties with lawyers or played softball with a group of women she'd known from her high school menstrual initiation classes.

The crescent initiation scar on her left wrist – I remembered seeing it years ago, but I didn't know how she got it. She had a tattoo as well, on her left hip, a blindfolded woman dancing on a purple flower. Where did she get it? Why? How long had she had it? Did it come from her bar enactment when she became a lawyer? Or something I knew nothing about? Maybe she'd gone skiing once and got caught in an avalanche, and after the dogs found her and the mountain crews nursed her back to health she inscribed the tattoo in a ceremony of recognition. I could have asked her; she would have told me, I'm sure. But I didn't want to ask. I wanted to know.

I didn't even know if she'd always been a lesbian, if she'd been a lesbian when I first met her. I didn't know when and how she'd come out, if she'd run away from home when she was seventeen to be initiated in a Women's World community outside Columbus, Ohio (I knew where she'd grown up, where she'd gone to school), or if she dated men, a few or a lot, gotten married, maybe had children (the idea of children horrified me; an ex-husband I could handle, but not children), and one day left with a fellow lawyer, the two of them going on pilgrimage to a woman's beach where they washed themselves free of their former lives.

At one point, in the middle of licking her thigh actually, I suddenly thought of her friend Jack. What did it mean when she said they 'lived together for a while' (see, I remembered her exact words, I would have been a good lawyer after all)? Did she mean *lived* together or just shared an apartment? I wanted to stop, put her thigh on hold, and ask all about Jack. But even apart from the issue of stopping, how could I ask about Jack who got himself killed? Who had brought us together, the way Paul had brought us together?

And I didn't want to stop. I didn't want to stop ever. I

wanted to lick her thighs, her hips, the creases of her legs
meeting her groin, the folds of her lips, her clitoris, her
wonderful shy clitoris and the never-ending wetness inside
her. I wanted to do everything I'd never allowed myself to
think about, not with Alison Birkett, the hero-villain of my
childhood. I wanted to go on and on, to have her kiss my
face, my neck, my shoulders and down to my breasts, with
her hand deep inside me the whole time, gently rocking,
the fingers moving in waves. I didn't want to think that she
had longed for these things as much as I had, that she had
thought about them, wondering what I looked like, how
I had 'turned out', who I'd become, did I even like girls,
and what would she have done if I hadn't? (In the middle
of all these thoughts I realized that I trusted her, I never
questioned it when she said that she had kept away from
me all those ten years, hadn't checked up on me.) And I
didn't want to think that maybe she'd even planned for all
of this, meticulous ethical behaviour or not. Planned how I
didn't know, but I didn't want even to look at the idea.

We did stop of course, time and again, to talk, to ask
each other about our lives, to laugh – at one point I
said something to her about her casual elegance and
she threw back her head, laughing really loudly, then
told me how the first time she'd gone out looking for
me she'd tried on five or six outfits before settling on the
'casual' combination I'd finally seen. We stopped to eat
(I called out for vegetable dumplings and shrimp in black
bean sauce, and then Alison took the phone and talked
the restaurant owner into having his delivery boy stop at
a liquor store for a bottle of champagne). We stopped for
Alison to look at some of my work and for me to ask about
some of her cases.

We didn't talk about what had brought us together. About
Lisa Black Dust Tunnel Light, or Senator Channing, or the
men and women in the tubular masks.

The hours got confused, speeding up or slowing down of
their own accord. But it was nearly midnight and we had

stopped once again to drink orange juice, when I knew it was time to get us past some of the traps that could bite us at any moment. I knew it was time because Alison had said something about pouring a stream of juice down my body and licking it up and I found myself shocked. Just a little, but enough to know I had to make a jump and she had to make it with me.

I stood up from the tiny table in my tiny kitchen. 'Alison,' I said, amazed at how nervous I was with this woman who had so recently been climbing inside my body, 'I would like to do an enactment with you.'

She stood up as well. Her face became grave and I panicked that I had done the wrong thing. But then she took off the purple satin robe I'd given her to wear (a present from an ex-lover, but I didn't feel she had to know that; she was wearing it open, draping the sides of her breasts) and inclined her head towards me in the way of someone accepting a spirit obligation. She held out her hand, palm up, for me to take it. Briefly, I thought of just pulling her to me and kissing her, but I knew I had to follow through on what I'd said. To proclaim an obligation and then abandon it is like slicing through a tenuous web that has only begun to take shape. So hand in hand and walking slightly apart, we marched into the bedroom, this time heading not to the bed, but to the screened-off part of the room where I had set up my true life altar.

The enactment was slow and graceful. Before I could move aside the screen, Alison insisted on touching it, spreading wide her fingers as she traced the paintings of the night sky and the waves, touching the beads and feathers and ribbons, carefully reading (she moved her lips) the texts I'd copied from Ingrid Burning Snake and Maryanna Split Sky and Li Ku Unquenchable Fire, while touching their photos, taped with shiny black Founder's Tape to the centre of the screen.

A pot of finger paste lay in front of the screen. Alison pointed to it and I nodded. Her designs were simple, abstract swirls for the most part, but I liked that she used both hands, and especially that she allowed herself to paint over some of my designs, even touching the photos of the Founders with dots of paint, as if to acknowledge that the place of 'Ellen alone' was about to change, that I had invited her to change it. 'All right,' she said finally, and let me accordion the screen aside.

For years I'd been collecting and making materials to use in some special enactment, when I would know it really counted. I had no idea what it would be (well, at first I thought I would do it when I met Mr Right, but I soon gave that up), only that I didn't entirely trust anything from the SDA, and at some point I would want my own ingredients. Now I kneeled by a large wooden box covered in sea shells and small pebbles I'd pasted on, one by one, over a couple of years. When I opened the lock (a gold-plated lion, with the key sliding into its roaring mouth) and lifted the lid, I could almost hear a whisper of voices, excited at being called to action.

Before Alison could enter I needed to lay out a true ground. For this I used a rope made of strips of cloth torn from the clothes I'd worn at different primary enactments throughout my childhood, starting with the feathered blanket the midwives had given me for my rising into my newborn body. My mother had given me all these things when I'd left home to go to college. I'm sure she'd have approved of me putting them safely in a chest – but not ripped to pieces. With the rope I set out the lines of a true ground on the floor, careful to keep it curved at all points for the female body.

Within this field I laid down a silk scarf, golden and turquoise, for the Sun and the Sea, the light of knowledge shining on the sullen mysteries of the soul. Broken pieces of chains held down the silk, a sign of liberation for Chained Mother, held prisoner at the bottom of the ocean.

Next came a 'standing announcement', a metal pole

I'd made, with branches hung with downward pointing triangles. The triangles were made of red velvet on wire frames, decorated with yellow and indigo ribbons. In the centre the largest triangle was a double layer of black velvet, with a space between the layers for a small revolving light and a tape loop. The light shone through a gauzy red vertical strip down the centre of the triangle. On the outside of this strip I'd pasted folds of pink satin to suggest labia. The tape loop, set up on a miniaturized cassette player (another boon from Radio Temple), consisted of women moaning in soft joy. A single wire fed electricity to both the light and the tape. The wire plugged into one of two sockets in the apartment officially sanctified to receive sacred current. So I guess I couldn't escape SDA involvement after all.

When I turned on the tape and the light Alison grinned at me. I could see she wanted to say something, or maybe even do something inspired by the moaning triangle, but she kept silent, allowing me to go ahead. There were several other things to set out, including a small fan which plugged into the other half of the sacred socket. I'd painted the four blades of the fan with dots, concentric circles, mouths and my handprint. Before I set it going I asked Alison to dip her hand in the black paste and place her print over mine. When I turned on the switch the blades moved around slowly, just enough to billow the cloth.

The final participants didn't come from the box, but from my shelf of permanent house guardians above the regular altar. These were three clay statues, rough images of women I'd made from mud collected after a storm on a song journey I'd made in the Adirondack mountains shortly after I left college. I'd painted them in thick globs of paste, one yellow, one red and one black. I set them on the floor in a row, but when I straightened up Alison bent down before the guardians to remove the protection from around her neck and slip it over the head of the one in the middle, the black. I touched her shoulder and looked at her as she stood up. I think I was crying, I'm not even sure. This small silver and gold cylinder was refuge, the place where she kept the external bodies of her real self. She had made herself naked for me, willing to start over, and she had shown me that that was the point of what we were doing, to allow ourselves a new beginning, naked and fresh. We had to offer the relationship we used to have, because we could not just build on that, and at the same time we had to cherish it, even the people who had died in the making of it.

I was about to invite Alison into the circle with me when she held up a hand, the one still dark with paste from the handprint, and darted into the kitchen, coming back with an apple and a knife. I smiled and nodded at her and then we entered together.

I closed my eyes and took a breath as I always do when I enter an opening to the Living World. The fan blew on my legs and I could smell a sharpness in the air as I breathed deeply, taking life and Alison into my blood. When I opened my eyes she was looking at me. We kissed each other and moved our hands in slow loose waves up and down each other's bodies, lowering ourselves until we were kneeling on the silk floor, our bodies pressed together. The revolving light moved on and off her face, searching her out, while the number of women moaning on the tape seemed to increase with every turn of the loop.

With my hands I guided Alison to lie down on the ground, where I stroked her in one long movement from her forehead to her toes, sweeping off all the strains and residues she'd brought with her from the outside. Speaking very softly I told her the story of Maryanna Split Sky, how the day after the Parade of the Animals in Pasadena, the masked children's riot that sparked the Revolution, Split Sky lay down naked in the main street of her town, offering her body as an opening to the Living World so that the Revolution might truly begin. I repeated for her that story we all know, how when the police came a wind blew them back, and when the TV people tried to badger her their cameras broke, how her body glowed like molten rock, like the Earth in its infancy, and how the sky filled with grey clouds, becoming like stone, weighing people down to their knees, until Maryanna shouted and the stone sky split open with light and rain, all at the same time.

Alison pulled me down on top of her and we began to make love, sliding up and down each other's bodies, sometimes lifted into the air by the breath of the fan, sometimes as heavy as the three clay women who watched over us. When we sat up again, Alison took the apple and the knife, her own enactment knife I saw, a small brass blade with a handle the shape of a tortoise. I realized I didn't know where she'd got it, what meaning the tortoise held for her, if it represented some secret society of lawyers, or an encounter with a slow-moving helper on some private adventure in the woods somewhere or maybe a sanctified zoo or refuge. And I realized too that it didn't matter, she would tell me, I would learn all these things.

Alison cut the apple across the middle, revealing the five-pointed star in each half. As we sat twined around each other like strands of DNA, eating our stars, the moaning on the tape changed to laughter and the fan began to sing, while Alison and I and the three clay ladies all hummed happily along.

5

Alison and I met with Alexander Timmerman four days later. It had taken us that long to get through the layers of bureaucrats, hangers-on and probably government spies and obstructionists just to talk to him and persuade him that we had something to tell him. During the whole process I had to remind myself about twenty times that the government would find out whatever it wanted to about our negotiations, so we might as well not try to hide them.

Timmerman met us in a large living room style office, with grey chairs and a couch facing twentieth-floor corner windows overlooking lower Manhattan. Appearing slightly smaller up close than on a platform, Timmerman gestured at the room with his hand, as if to make it disappear in some political stage trick. 'I'm sorry about all this,' he said. 'The PR people tell me I have to live up to my status.' He offered us spring water from a plain glass pitcher, pouring it into glasses with the logo for Consumer Liberation.

'I have to confess something,' he said. 'I've been feeling secretly giddy ever since Martin – my secretary – told me that Alison Birkett wanted to see me. I still remember the way you forced the government's hand on the Pentagon possession. It was one of the things that eventually inspired me to give up corporate law and seek guidance on what service the Living World wanted me to perform.' He didn't mention Alison's later accusation of Malignant temp agencies under contract to the White House. In gratitude, I stopped myself from asking if he'd framed any pictures of her from *Time* magazine.

When Alison had thanked him and shown her interest in his work by citing a couple of his lesser-known triumphs, he turned to me, said how pleased he was to meet me and asked if I was part of Ms Birkett's firm. I disappointed him, and Alison added that 'Ms Pierson and I work on special projects together.'

Alison laid it out for him, only leaving out her personal connection to Jack Chikowsky, the way we'd found out about Margaret Light-at-the-End-of-the-Tunnel 23's connection to Arthur Channing and our knowledge of her previous incarnation. We'd discussed that last point for some time, wondering if we might need it to shock Timmerman into recognizing that he was being set up. Finally, we decided that it raised too many issues of our own involvement.

Timmerman listened carefully, sometimes with his head down, sometimes looking sharply at Alison or me. Pretty soon it became clear that he did not want to hear what we were telling him. When Alison told him about Jack, and about the other incidents, he nodded and said how tragic that was and how he'd asked the Twins (he didn't call them that) to channel their blessings into more gentle manifestations. When we suggested that these events suggested some sort of conspiracy, he smiled and asked, 'A conspiracy to do what? Make people feel happy? I'm very sorry if occasionally some people have had trouble handling their own joy, but I find it hard to accept that an ecstatic blessing can be a plot. If anything, the problems simply show how much people need the experience, so that it would not come as such a shock to their starved systems.' I asked him if it didn't strike him as odd that none of this got into the press. He said, 'That sounds more like people caring about our cause than people wanting to hurt us.'

We had to do some dodging of our own, for Timmerman seemed more concerned about what we knew about the banking issue than any of the subjects we wanted to raise. For a while, he and Alison danced around each other, struggling over whose agenda would dominate the discussion – his to find out what we knew of Channing's banking connections, Alison's to focus on the Being summoned by Carolyn Park-Wu. After a few minutes, Alison convinced him that we had not concerned ourselves with the details of his investigations, only the fact that he clearly was on to something, and that it was Arthur Channing who had sent Tunnel Light to him.

'Of course we knew that our Friend came to us from Senator Channing,' he told us. 'And we are not naive, believe me, not after all our campaigns. If Senator Channing is hoping to influence us away from our investigations by bringing Margaret to us, then *he* is certainly naive and can expect a few shocks. But I suspect you know that, or have guessed.'

'May I ask a question?' I said. I could still put on innocence when I needed it, and was still young enough to make it work. 'What exactly does Margaret Light-at-the-End-of-the-Tunnel 23 do for you?'

'She gives us support,' he said. 'She strengthens us to do what we need to do. I realize that may sound a little vague to you, but if you've ever experienced the presence of a Bright Being in your life, you will understand that strength is not a vague or empty concept at all. Not at all.'

I said, 'How can you know that she is not doing something to you that you can't detect? Something that will weaken your work rather than support it?'

'Because she's Benign, Ms Pierson. Don't you think we had her checked? And not by the SDA, either. She cannot *help* but look after our best interests.'

It was right around then that Maggie Tunnel Light came in and joined us.

With her heavily made up eyes, her pale skin and black hair, she looked much the same as she had in Miracle Park, except that she wore no lipstick and this time she was all in white, a shapeless tunic over straight-legged white pants. Only her sandals were coloured, the same shade of soft green as the office carpet, giving her a look of some albino flower rising from the grass. 'I am Alexander's Friend,' she said, and sat down beside him on the couch.

I couldn't help myself. Hardly knowing I was saying it I half whispered, 'Ferocious One, I beg you to release me. I know that—'

I didn't get any further. I'm not sure if I stopped because I was shaking too hard to speak, or because of Maggie's reaction. She sat back, wincing as if I'd slapped her, and said to Timmerman, her voice breaking slightly, 'Alexander, what is she doing?'

Timmerman said, 'Ms Pierson! This is a Benevolent Being, an emissary,' but neither Alison nor I paid him any attention. We looked at each other, each of us thinking the same thing. *She doesn't know. She doesn't realize she's ever been anything else.*

Now that I'd stopped, the Being had regained her composure. She touched Timmerman's shoulder, saying, 'It's all right. I will help them.'

Later, Alison and I talked about those next moments. The terrible thing was we knew what was happening, what she was doing, and there was no way we could stop it. A sweetness was opening inside us, a feeling that all the restrictions that clamped us so tightly were falling away, that we could really breathe for the first time in our lives, everything could open up to its full size, all the broken pieces were flowing together. We were in love, wasn't that enough, why did we need to worry about anything else? When it passed, after about fifteen seconds, I discovered myself sweating, staring at the floor with my hands clenched.

I discovered I had lowered my head. When I looked up, Tunnel Light was leaning back with her hands pressed together in her lap and Timmerman had his arms crossed. 'Do you see?' he said. 'Is there any doubt as to her intentions?'

She turned to him. 'Alexander,' she said, 'maybe I should speak to them.'

'Of course,' he said, and stood up. 'Ms Birkett,' he said, 'I really do feel honoured. And I appreciate your and Ms Pierson's concern. Honestly. But believe me, it's misplaced. We do know what we're doing. Trust us.' He held out his hand and we stood up to shake it.

The three of us remained on our feet after Timmerman left. There was a moment of silence, punctured only by my own noisy breathing which I couldn't seem to get under control, and then Alison said, 'Whatever you're going to do to us, I want you to know that it doesn't matter. You can make us feel, or think, what you want right now, but it will wear off. And we will keep pushing, I promise you that.'

She shook her head. 'You don't understand. I don't want to control you. I came here to help.'

I could feel myself yearning to believe her, to just drop everything and go off with Alison. We could go back to my apartment, switch on the blessing fan and let its breezes stir the waters in us as we lay in the bed. I made myself think of Paul, of the snakes in the elevator. 'Help us how?' I said.

She took a half step forward. 'You are frightened that I have come to harm Alexander. To sabotage his work. But I tell you that his work does not concern me. I help him in any way I can, but that is not why I am here.' She seemed to be looking only at me; when I asked Alison later, she had felt the same thing. Tunnel Light said, 'Human beings are starving. Your souls need a special kind of nourishment, the release of ecstasy found in sexual expression. I tell you this freely. I have come here to help humans fulfil their sexual hunger. Are you shocked? You should not be. You yourselves *know* this. You have let yourselves taste a small portion of what is possible for you.'

Alison's hand took hold of mine; or maybe it was the other way around. She was shaking as she held on tightly to me. The Being went on, 'Humans starve themselves because of their fear. You live in a culture which teaches you to lock yourselves away from your bodies and everything that can release them. My purpose here is simple. I only want to help you overcome your own starvation.'

Alison said, 'Your kind of food is killing people. It's too strong.'

Tunnel Light nodded. 'I accept that we have made mistakes. Sometimes we have acted too quickly. That will change. But we will not change our purpose.'

'Why Timmerman?' I asked. 'Why not, oh, the Congress? Or the Revolutionary Republican Party?'

'Alexander seeks liberation,' she said. 'He seeks many different forms of liberation, many of which do not concern us. However, he includes among these the liberation of sexual expression. And he provides a way for the Beings to touch the people who come to his rallies. They come just for that touch. We give them something to hold within them, like a quick-spreading virus, one that heals instead of hurts. It is possibly a small thing, but it helps, if only in a small way.'

Alison said, 'Do you know how you came to Timmerman in the first place?'

She shrugged. The motion was small, delicate. 'Carolyn Park-Wu summoned me.'

'And gave you your purpose?'

Tunnel Light shook her head. 'She dedicated me to Alexander. For that I am grateful to her, whatever her own motives were. My purpose is my own.'

I thought, which means that they built the purpose into the configuration itself. She can't be dissuaded. It's part of her nature.

Alison said, 'And you know that Park-Wu works for Arthur Channing, and that your Alexander is investigating Channing?'

'Of course. I told you, those issues do not concern me. And I have told you that I will do nothing to hurt Alexander. Whatever plan Park-Wu may have expected me to fulfil, I will disappoint her. I do not serve Carolyn Park-Wu, I serve Alexander Timmerman. Why won't you accept that?'

I thought, because we know who you really are. But she didn't. All the way down, she believed in herself as Margaret Light-at-the-End-of-the-Tunnel 23. Could they have planted some sort of suggestion in her, ready to turn her back into Lisa Black Dust 7 at the right moment?

I said, 'Suppose a Malignant One could take your place with Timmerman. Maybe Channing has some method to dislodge you now that Timmerman trusts you. What could it do?'

Her face crinkled and she looked in genuine pain. 'That cannot happen,' she said.

'Humour me. You want to protect him, don't you? If Channing has some scheme, shouldn't we try to anticipate it? What could a Malignant One do to him? In your position.'

'Stop it!' she shouted, and I jumped back, my face scalded, my chest feeling like something had smashed into it.

Alison put her arms around me. Her body felt a little shaky, but she managed to keep her shoulders back as she looked at Tunnel Light. 'Please forgive her,' she said. 'She doesn't understand that you can hurt.' To me she said, 'You can't ask her to do that. Anticipate what a Ferocious One might do or plan. Thinking like the enemy is too painful for her.'

The pressure on my chest relaxed and I got myself upright. The enemy stood with her feet together and her hands clasped below her waist. She said, 'Be calm. I will not harm Alexander. It is not possible for me to do so. Nor will I allow anyone else to harm him. Alexander is safe.'

Alison and I didn't speak all the way down the stairs from Timmerman's office. When we reached the street, I started to say something until Alison put a hand on my arm. 'Not yet,' she said. A few blocks from Timmerman's office stood a Teller's Hall, one of those huge stone and stained-glass buildings from before the Revolution, a 'church' as it was called, converted to sacred space by Marion Firetongue, so that a statue of the Founder now stood just inside the doorway. We stepped into the dark open space, lit only by the daylight from the high windows. With our arms crossed over our chests and our hands on our shoulders, we touched our heads to the sides of the statue.

'Guard us and conceal us,' we said. 'Shield us and seal us from all alien presences.' Alison sighed as she stood up. 'Well,' she said, 'I guess we're about as safe from interference as we're going to get.'

Whatever the building's interior used to be had long since vanished when the Faceless Workers came and cleansed the city in the Time of Fanatics after the Revolution. Now, the great open space of the main hall had been transformed into a replica of the garden where the mysterious 'Uncle Jeffrey' had sat talking to Firetongue over five days and nights, persuading her to 'break the blood' – leave her family – and join the Army of the Saints. In the middle of the floor computer-animated statues of Firetongue and Jeffrey sat on a bench under a stone tree. They moved their heads side to side, constantly whispering. Alison and I sat on wooden chairs by a pair of small potted bushes off in the corner, ready at last for our own whispering.

The fact is, there wasn't all that much to say. I suggested

to Alison my idea of a pre-programmed switch at the right moment, Lisa Black Dust 7 re-emerging to destroy Timmerman. Alison said, 'I just don't see how they could do that. You can't just . . . hypnotize a Bright Being. For one thing, they don't have brains.'

'I feel like I don't either, at the moment. Look. Park-Wu summons the Being, sends her off to Timmerman, not as a servant of Channing or Park-Wu herself, but as a genuine helper for Timmerman. Which means that Tunnel Light can't hurt him. Or even let anyone else hurt him. She can only help. And yet, we know that Timmerman's on the verge of exposing Channing. And there must be a reason why they chose a reconfigured Black Dust 7. I will not believe that that is just some accident.'

She held my hand. 'I've gotten rusty at this, I'm afraid. In the old days I would have known better than to go to Timmerman without all the facts. That was stupid. I'm sorry.'

'I'm not doing any better,' I said. 'You know, Alison, it's a good thing you really didn't just want to see me for help on this Timmerman thing. You would have gone away pretty fed up.'

She grinned at me. 'I have to admit, I'm glad my hidden agenda was the one that got satisfied.' She stood up, still holding my hands. 'Come on,' she said. 'We're probably as safe outside as in here.'

We stood in the doorway, where I winced at the sun, the noise of the traffic and people. Looking at Alison, I wished I could kiss her, starting at the eyebrows and working my way down. She said, 'I'm just afraid things are coming to a head sooner than we know how to react. My guess is that Timmerman's about ready to move.'

I said, 'We could try to find out what he's planning. What Channing's involvement is.'

She shrugged. 'Then all we'd know is what Timmerman knows. We need to find out what he doesn't know. What Margaret-Lisa is going to do to him.'

'I wonder,' I said. Alison looked at me, waiting. 'I wonder if Tunnel Light herself knows what she's going to do.'

'What do you mean?'

'Well, maybe I'm fixated on this switch idea, but if she's really sincere – and you tell me she has no choice – then somehow she's going to do something to him without knowing she's doing it.'

'Like what?'

'I'm not sure. Maybe . . . maybe she'll stop him if he veers away from what she considers important. She obviously doesn't consider Channing of any significance. Maybe she's somehow . . . programmed in some way, to force Timmerman away from banking and back to sex.'

Alison was frowning, trying to assess what I was suggesting. She looked delicious and I found myself wanting to force *her* away from banking. She said, 'How would she force him? She can't hurt him.'

'She could sabotage what he's doing. That wouldn't hurt *him*.'

She shook her head. 'I still doubt it. Maybe I'm slightly fixated myself, but my understanding is that the compulsion to serve Timmerman would lead her to help him further his plans.'

'Even if it went against her plans?'

She tilted her head to the side, unconsciously causing her hair to fall slightly away from her face, into the sun. Straightening up, she said, 'I'll have to think about that. Maybe I can check on your idea about programming. Is it possible to dedicate a Bright Being in such a way that it reacts automatically to a specific situation?'

Feeling not very confident, I said, 'And I'll try to think about what exactly they might want to programme her to do.'

There was a pause, and then Alison said, 'Would you like to come over tonight?' There was something very sweet about her hesitancy, her caution about any assumptions. I said, 'Of course.'

She stroked my cheek. I closed my eyes and made some kind of purring noise. 'How about dinner?' Alison said. 'I'll cook. My cooking doesn't go much beyond roast chicken and yoghurt salad, but if you say nice things to me I'll try for some potato pancakes.'

'I'll start right now,' I said, and whispered suggestions of niceness in her ear. 'How about eight?' I asked. 'I think I need some time just to sit. Try to see whatever it is I'm not seeing.'

Alison quoted Adrienne Birth-of-Beauty, the Fifth Proposition from her Shout From the Skyscraper. 'See what there is to see. Hear what there is to hear. Touch whatever you touch. Speak the thing you must speak.'

'If I knew what it was,' I said, 'I'd be happy to speak it.'

But it wasn't Alison or even Birth-of-Beauty who opened me to what was there. It was Joan Monteil.

When the bell rang, around four that afternoon, my first thought was that my government had returned, wanting to tell me I shouldn't be hanging out in Teller Halls with Alison Birkett. But then I realized that the tube-faced people used their own keys, so I decided to ask over the intercom who it was. The usual indistinguishable scratchy voice came back. 'It's me. It's Joan Monteil. Joan? You know. Ellen? Let me in. There's so much . . . Let me in.'

Wishing I hadn't answered, I buzzed her through. I didn't want to face Joan right now. Every day since that first night with Alison I'd woken up thinking that I had to call Joan, tell her I couldn't see her any more, tell her I was sorry if I'd hurt her. The usual. Words that sound like a lie even when they're true. And every time other things came first. Timmerman was more urgent. Alison was more deserving.

The doorbell rang. And rang. And rang. Joan was

pressing it over and over, like some enactment prayer buzzer summoning people back into their bodies. When I opened the door she came rushing in, full of cheer. 'Ellen,' she said, in an odd breathy voice. 'Oh, Ellen, it's . . . it's just so wonderful to see you.' There was something strange about the way she looked, too. It took me a moment to realize just what it was. She had on very heavy makeup, but it wasn't like she'd put it on too thickly, it was more as if there were layers, as if she'd carefully done herself up, then decided she wasn't satisfied and did it all over again, except without removing the earlier layer. And then again. Her hair had a kind of matted overstyled look, yet disorganized, as if there too she couldn't seem to decide and just kept adding more and more gel, or spray, every time she decided to change it. As she talked, she moved around the apartment in a nervous dance, even pirouetting, with movements that tried to be graceful or provocative, but ended up as too abrupt, off balance. She had a habit of moving her fingers on her body, down her cheek, or along her thigh. She was dressed all in black, wearing stretch jeans and a T-shirt. I could only watch, confused and a little frightened. Now and then, she would come towards me, leaning forward, or putting out a hand to stroke my face. Without thinking, I pulled away from her.

'I dreamed about you,' she said. 'It was so incredible. I was eating. Fruit. Or soup? And everything was hot. All over me. I just wanted to climb into it. Stir it with my breasts. Isn't that great? Have you ever done that? Oh, you've done everything. I know. And *you* were in the dream. Part of the mirror. Did I tell you about the mirror? It was so dark, but you were breathing, I could hear you whisper to me, you were just whispering over and over and over, the same thing, how much you wanted me, and we could sink into the mirror. With the moon.' She came very close and began to move her fingernails across the top of my chest.

I lifted her hand away. 'Listen, Joan,' I started, but she wasn't listening.

'I took it down to NORA,' she said. 'I thought they should have it. To match it. With all the others. I know there's others, there has to be. All over. That's what she said. How we all deserve it. But not you, of course. I mean, not you in other people's dreams.' She giggled. 'Of course, you *deserve* it. You more than anyone.' She was touching things, running her hand along a lamp pole, or sliding an eraser between her palms, or moving her finger along a picture frame and then touching her lips. It reminded me of something.

'I've been meaning to call you—' I tried.

'Meaning!' she said. 'That's exactly what that bitch at NORA said. Mean, mean, mean, mean. What does it mean? Does it mean? I told her I know what it *means*, I just wanted to give it to her. Like you.'

The phone rang. Joan grunted, then opened her mouth into a wide O and made heavy breathing noises while I grabbed the phone and half shouted, 'Hello?'

Harry Astin's voice said, 'Well hi, Ellen. Glorybe and I were wondering—'

'Harry,' I said, 'get over here. Right now.' The moment I put the phone down Joan took it away from me, lifting the whole thing up and swinging her leg over the wire like someone getting onto a horse. She began to move the wire around her thighs and back and forth in her crotch, then rubbed the entire phone in large circles over her belly. 'Have you ever done this? Have you done this? Oh, stupid. Of course. You're Ellen. You're Ellen. You've done everything.'

'Joan,' I said, 'let's sit down.'

She threw the phone on the floor, laughing as the bell sounded. 'What?' she said. 'What should we sit on?' She came towards me suddenly and began to move her leg up and down against mine. I stepped back and she followed me, then abruptly stopped to pick up a silver turtle guardian my mother had given me and rub it around the front of her body, making soft laughing noises as she did it.

That was when I realized what she reminded me of. The people at Alexander Timmerman's rally, the ones who'd received the blessing and couldn't stop touching things. I tried to think of any Timmerman events Joan might have attended, but I knew he hadn't done anything public, certainly not in this area, since the park.

'Joan,' I said, 'listen to me. I need you to tell me if you've—'

'Tell, tell, tell,' Joan chanted. She laughed. 'I won't tell if you won't tell. Do you fuck and tell? Do you like to tell?' She began to march around the room, picking things up, rubbing them against her body, offering them to me, dropping them, sliding against other objects, pictures, the walls, the corners of desks or the backs of chairs.

'You don't know what you're doing,' I tried to tell her, but she wasn't interested. She came at me, dashing forward, just touching her fingers all over me, whatever she could reach, sometimes sliding the whole hand, other times jabbing me with her fingertips or scratching me with her nails. 'Stop it,' I tried to tell her. Any time I backed up she pursued me, pushing me backwards, until I found myself against the wall, where Joan began first to kiss me, any place she could reach, and then to bite, small jabs with her teeth. She was making animal noises, not real ones, but the kind of cute sounds children learn in kindergarten songs.

I pushed her away, harder than I thought, so that she fell back against the desk. When she recovered her balance she leaned forward, hands on her knees, and shouted at me. 'What do you want? Do you want me to fuck you? Fuck you? Fuck you? Like your law-yer bitch? Is that the idea? I'll do it, I'll do what-ever you like, I'll fuck you so hard you'll split right open and everything will spill out, just like you did to me.'

'Joan!' I said. 'You've got to listen to me. You don't know what you're doing.'

She laughed, rubbing circles on her crotch. 'Lawyer talk, counsellor? Why don't you take me? Don't you want it? It's free. No billable hours.'

I darted around her, managed to reach my altar, where I grabbed hold of the three guardians, the ones I'd set out for my enactment with Alison, along with the can of flash powder and a box of sanctified matches. I wanted more tools, but there was no time and it was just so hard to think straight.

I tried to set the guardians out in a triangle enclosing Joan and I, but I should have known it was hopeless. As soon as I set them up she kicked them over. 'What are you going to do?' she said. 'Buy me off with your sluts?' She picked up the one painted black and rubbed it over her breasts, then between her legs. 'Oh,' she said, as if surprised. 'This is just like *her*, isn't it? Has she been here? Is she going to come through the wall? Are the walls going to come?' She laughed, then pushed the statue hard at her crotch. 'Right through the fucking walls,' she said.

'Joan,' I said, 'she's not your friend. Please believe me. Anything you get from her is not a gift. She's the *enemy*, Joan. The enemy. You've got to get her out of you.'

She flung the guardian at me, or maybe just at the wall, since if she was throwing it at me, she missed by more than a foot. The clay husk shattered and I could feel the spirit who'd been living inside it hover in the air, confused, and then drift away. I wanted to cry, but there was no time. I could invite her back later, or properly say goodbye.

Joan was going through my night table, throwing things on the floor. I began to lay down the flash powder, trying to do it without her noticing. It wasn't difficult. She had found what she was looking for, the penetrator-resonator set she'd given me, and now was moving the penetrator around her face with one hand, while she hung on to its bird-headed sister with the other. 'Let's make it sing,' she said. 'Can we make it sing now? Sing?' She began to hum in imitation of the bird while continuing to move the fish woman all over her body.

The flash of the powder going off made her cry out and drop the resonator on the floor. She shook her head, then yelped as if I'd hurt her when I set off another pile of powder. 'Ellen?' she said. 'Why are you . . . let's sing. Let's make everything . . . She told me you were hungry. She told me we could both feed on her, feed on her.'

I set off another flash and then reached around her for the feathers and salt I'd used after the tube people had left. I threw the salt on her and began waving the feathers, trying to think what I needed to say. I don't remember exactly, but it went something like 'Powers of protection and harmony, empty this woman, clean her of invasion and pollution. Send all Malignant and Benign Beings away from her. Seal her and . . .' I couldn't say 'bless her' because that's what Benign Ones are supposed to do. And she had *been* blessed. Lamely, I said, 'Seal her and free her.'

Joan grabbed a feather out of my hand. When she moved it over my face I turned my head. Dropping it, she began to shake her head. 'Ellen?' she said. 'Don't you . . . Ellen, this is . . . is it her? Is it her? I've got so much, so much, I dreamed about us—' She stopped, turned her head. The doorbell was ringing.

'Harry,' I said, opening it. 'Oh God, thank you for getting here.'

It took Harry and I an hour to cool Joan down enough to take her to a clinic of the Inner Spirit, over on Avenue C. Harry was wonderful. He just took her hands and started to dance around the apartment with her, a kind of cheerful square dance skipping and loping, the whole time telling her a stream of gossip about office politics and his upstairs neighbour. When suddenly her knees gave way and she fell down, he sat beside her and began whispering to her, getting her finally to close her eyes and lean against him while I got my mid-winter initiation cloak to put over her in case she went into shock.

Harry wanted to take her to a hospital, but I told him we couldn't go anywhere with SDA connections. He didn't argue. At the clinic a Ragged Healer received Joan, waving me away when I tried to tell her what the problem was. The healer, a woman I think, wore a mask of ribbons and strings of beads that covered much of her face. The beads were money, I knew, legal tender in the spirit worlds where she would travel to bring back the scattered pieces of Joan's soul. On her robe, a heavy shapeless mass of unbleached cotton, fur strips and plastic panels, she carried, among all her other equipment, a small computer screen showing exchange rates for spirit currencies. Several other screens showed images of the room itself, but oddly distorted, either broken down into dots, or with narrow tunnel vision, or filled with pulsating colours. Harry later suggested to me that these might be animal perceptions of the world, the viewpoints of her various animal spirit helpers and fellow travellers. The robe also held keys, bells, a saw and hammer, a miniature flashlight, a hand-sized pinball machine, a fish-shaped water gun, a box of classroom chalk, a group of very small dolls on a metal ring, goggles, eyeglasses with eyes painted on them, and several cans of 35 mm film without a camera. When we formally gave Joan to her care, she handed us several business cards, each with some sort of prophetic image – a volcano exploding, a snake licking a flower, birds eating a carcass – and words in some incomprehensible script.

To my surprise, the healer, who couldn't have been more than five feet six inches, picked Joan up in her arms, all the while murmuring to her, and carried her to the centre of the room, where she set her down in a jewelled circle. With the various chalk she drew a series of concentric circles around Joan, representations of the various worlds she would travel through to reach Joan:

the Earth, the Sky, the Sun, Moon and Stars, the Land of the Dead, and the worlds of her various spirit helpers. The rounded corners of the room glowed with wavy lines of neon light, a physical picture of the Living World.

Harry pulled me away from the doorway as the healer began swaying back and forth and singing very softly – snatches of old songs, I think, particularly 'Oh Susanna' and 'My Old Kentucky Home'.

'Let's go, sweetie,' Harry said to me.

'Shouldn't we make sure it's really helping?' I whispered.

'We'll just get in the way. Maybe suck something up ourselves. Or cause a backlash. And you know it can take hours. Or days.' I let him lead me away, only looking back briefly at the healer shining her flashlight towards the ceiling as she moved her head from side to side.

In the street, Harry put an arm around me and stroked my cheek. 'She'll be fine,' he said.

Moving away from him, I sighed and shook my head. 'Thanks,' I told him. 'I don't know . . . I just—' I took a deep breath. 'That was my fault, Harry. She's in all that spirit shit because of me.'

He took out his prosthetic cigarette from the pocket of his striped blazer. He tilted back his head to blow pretend smoke. 'Are you going to stop having sex with people because of the danger of possession? Ellen, Ellen, I find it hard to envision you turning your clothes inside out and joining a chastity support group.'

'It's not that,' I said.

'Then what? Your insincerity? The fact that you were using her? Don't you think she was using you? Perhaps one should not speak ill of the possessed, but Joan Monteil is an emotional masturbator.'

I took his arm and began moving him down the street. 'Harry,' I said, 'let's go get some coffee. I need to talk with you.'

'A conversation with you is always a delight.'

I laughed. 'Thanks. The thing is, it's kind of dangerous. What happened to Joan – it didn't happen because of the sex. That was part of it, but it involves a lot more. I'm scared, Harry. Scared for me, and . . .'

'Your old family friend. Alison Birkett, wasn't it?'

I stopped. 'You sonofabitch,' I said, laughing. 'Did you just remember her from that time on the street, or—'

He smiled at me, radiantly. Harry can do a great radiance. 'Darling,' he said, 'I knew who you were when I first met you. It was very thrilling, let me tell you. Ellen Pierson! I thought to myself. You were a hero of mine when I was a teenager.'

'You never said anything.'

He waved the hand with the cigarette. 'You didn't seem very eager to discuss it.'

I looked down. 'Yeah. Thanks, Harry.' Raising my head again, I said, 'But then you know the kind of thing that can happen around me and Alison. I don't want you hurt, Harry.'

'Well,' he said, 'I suspect you did not take Joan into your deepest confidence and that did not seem to protect her. So if I'm going to be in danger, I might as well know why.' He tilted his head back to blow imaginary smoke. 'Besides, what would life be without adventure?'

We went to a pita parlour on Avenue A, where Harry ordered hummus and I had coffee. I told him everything, or at least everything about Timmerman, ending with, 'I know the answer is right there, and I just feel so stupid that I can't see what's going to happen.'

Harry called the waitress as she went by and ordered tea and halvah. When the woman had gone, he leaned forward. 'Maybe you're a trifle fixated,' he said.

'What do you mean?'

'Well, you see this Margaret Tunnel Light and all you can think of is the Ferocious One who killed your cousin. So even though you accept that she will not directly harm Timmerman, you still assume that she will in some way attack him.' I thought of how I'd said to Alison that maybe Tunnel Light would do something to Timmerman without knowing what she was doing and how I'd assumed that meant a kind of programming. Harry went on, 'The point is this, Ellen. You know that Timmerman is being set up. Played for a patsy. But maybe Ms Light is being set up as well. Maybe they've taken this rather impressionable Bright Being and are playing her for a patsy as much as Timmerman.'

I leaned back and put a hand over my face, closing my eyes. I could hear the waitress setting down Harry's halvah, but I paid no attention. I was remembering the Being telling Alison and me, 'Alexander is safe'. But what of Consumer Liberation? What of his plans? Channing didn't care about Timmerman personally, he cared about the plan to expose the banking system. I'd been assuming that Tunnel Light would have to betray her trust. But suppose she did something with all her good intentions and with no intent at all to harm Timmerman – but that was the effect? Did she think she was harming Joan? Did she possess Joan and send her to me to attack me? It struck me that Maggie Tunnel Light probably thought she was helping us. Showing us the potential of her gifts to humanity. She was insane, I realized. I didn't know if you could use such terms for a Bright Being, but I thought how I could come up with few things scarier than an insane Devoted One.

'Alexander is safe,' she'd said. And something else. 'It is possibly a small thing.' The blessings, the frenzied arousal. These were possibly a small thing. What if she wanted to do something bigger? Some act of sexual liberation so overwhelming, so dramatic, it finally would make it into the newspapers and all the television stations. Suppose she was waiting for the proper moment. Some moment when all attention was focused on Timmerman.

I opened my eyes. 'Harry,' I said, 'she could do something horrible and think she was helping humanity.

She could "aid" Timmerman in such a way that she tore him to pieces. And if she "helped" him enough no one would ever listen to him again.' I felt a kind of awe for the simplicity of it. I'd been looking for tricks and surprises, but in fact the whole thing just hinged on the single-minded stupidity of divine benevolence.

I took hold of Harry's hands. 'Sweetheart,' I said, 'I've got to go speak to Alison. I can't tell you how much I thank you. For Joan, for being so smart, for just helping me face these things. For letting me keep my secrets. I can't tell you how good you are to me.'

Harry leaned back and smiled happily. With his pc in the corner of his mouth, he sucked in air, then blew it out. 'I will assume the check,' he said. 'You go see your friend. Glorybe and I will stand proudly on the sidelines while you overthrow the government.'

'I wish I could just laugh at that,' I said, and kissed him on the cheek.

There was a phone in the back, between the men's and women's toilets. I found myself looking around to make sure no one was nearby, then realized how meaningless that was. They could be following me, they could have microphones everywhere, including this phone line, they could masquerade as anybody. I wasn't even sure who 'they' were. The government? Devoted Ones? Malignant Ones? It seemed to me that we could hope for two things. If the government wanted to get rid of us they could do so at any time, whatever systems Alison had set up. So probably they did not take us seriously. And as for the Bright Beings, well, I had to hope that Channing couldn't bring in any Malignant Ones without confusing their Benign Friends. And that the Benign Ones would not directly try to harm us. Against their nature. I just prayed to all of *my* guardians that they wouldn't try to *help* us, the way they'd tried to help Joan.

When I announced myself to Alison's secretary she told

me, 'Oh, Ms Pierson. Thank you for calling. Ms Birkett has been trying to reach you.'

'Ellen,' Alison said when she came on the line. 'You've heard the news.'

'No,' I said. 'No. What news?'

'Timmerman's ready to go public. He's gotten permission to do an enactment in honour of Rebecca Rainbow inside the New York Stock Exchange. With a promise of live network television. This is where he makes his charges public, Ellen. I'm convinced of it.'

I said, 'And this is where they destroy him.'

'What?'

'I know what they're going to do,' I said. 'I know exactly what they're going to do. I just don't know what the goddamn hell we can do to stop them.'

6

Standing in the visitors' gallery above the trading floor, looking down through the thick glass, I was struck most by how crowded the stock market was. Not just the people, some of whom were frantically making deals and filling quotas in the final minutes before Timmerman and his entourage would enter, others of whom had given up all thought of business as they milled around, telling jokes, pounding drums covered in bills, eating sandwiches, or just standing alone or in groups, looking up towards Rebecca Rainbow's body, suspended in her glass coffin above the business floor, or else towards the dark red bell in its glass cage, also high above the floor against the back wall. Beyond the dense and nervous crowd, equipment filled the room – clusters of phones on poles or in banks, spiritual supply posts where traders could find flash powder, paper enactment robes, representation dolls and other SDA-approved paraphernalia for last-minute help on some important deal, and especially the trading posts themselves.

There was something very animal-like about the trading posts. In the centre of each stood a huge dark box, painted over with spirit emblems for prosperity and containing the computer circuitry that linked all the deals. Thick poles containing cables rose from these boxes to join a maze of latticework just below the gold-embossed ceiling. Artbirds hung on thin wires from the latticework, a whole flock of the life-like bright birds, their voice circuits set for songs of wealth and harmony. Timmerman had wanted to set loose genuine pigeons so that Rainbow might speak through them but, according to Alison's contacts, the SDA refused to disrupt the calculated songs of the artbirds.

From the central cable box, each trading post opened out in a figure eight of counterspace where the actual work got done. The counters too were packed with people and equipment. Above the counters double banks of video screens showed the various transactions. Smaller video monitors hung just over the heads of the crowd on the ends of metal poles which extended out and downwards from the larger videos. The poles looked like legs, giving the dozen or so trading posts the appearance of giant insects swarming over the floor, about to attack the humans, small and vulnerable beneath them.

Above it all, in the visitors' gallery, squeezed in among the crowds swarming to watch Alexander Timmerman put on a show, I felt alone with myself despite the press of people. I'd brought my own special protection, a whole bag full of power objects given to me by Annie-O, who'd met me the day before in the Wild Refuge of Inner Wood Park at the northern tip of Manhattan. The bag was large – a leather satchel – and heavy from a group of rocks Annie had included. I held it against my chest while the room filled up behind me.

I thought of Alison, constantly on the phone, trying for the past three days to reach somebody, anyone who would listen to us and could somehow do something to stop what was going to happen. I thought of our efforts to reach Timmerman himself and the information from his staff that he had gone deep travelling and no one could bring him out of his meditations until the day of the enactment. And the clear message that they could hardly spare any time for absurd conspiracy theories of sabotaged enactments and manipulated Devoted Ones. So now I was here, by myself, with Alison still at her office, still trying to stop it any way she could, and I just knew she wouldn't succeed, Timmerman would march or dance confidently into the trap. And I found myself just watching, a spectator like everyone around me.

Maybe my detachment came from all the waiting, with Timmerman not yet in the building and nothing happening other than a few exchange workers putting on masks or enactment robes over their colour-coded jackets. Or maybe it was my relief that I'd gotten through the moment I'd dreaded most of all – meeting Paul. Halfway down Broad Street on my way to the visitors' entrance, I'd almost turned back when I'd realized I would have to take an elevator, that there was no way I could talk the tourist guides into unlocking the emergency stairs.

In the lobby as well, I'd just stood there, with my official visitor's pass crunched in my hand, wondering what the point of my watching was if I couldn't do anything, and why didn't I just go home, and what would Alison say if I couldn't face it. Finally, I told myself it was only the third floor, it wouldn't take more than ten seconds. I waited until the car had filled up, then slipped in before the door closed.

The last time I'd ridden in an elevator, the day I'd decided that I would keep healthier if I just took the stairs everywhere, the building super – it was Harry's apartment building, actually – had let the husk – Paul's husk – run down. The nylon 'hair' had mostly fallen off, the eye dots had rubbed out and kids had covered the pole itself with their own gang enactment signs. I remember how I'd wanted to trap that goddamn super in the elevator and bang his head against the door and scream at him, 'That's my cousin!' Instead, I'd just stopped riding in elevators.

Now, when I saw the polished steel, the actual jewels used for eyes, what looked like real human hair, I couldn't decide if I was relieved or more enraged. Instead, I looked away, unable to let him see me. And then it was over and I was upstairs by the lobby outside the visitors' gallery, and

I didn't have to worry about it again until the time came to go down.

Though the thick glass of the gallery made it impossible to actually hear anything down on the floor, the operators of the Exchange had set up loudspeakers for us to hear the enactment and Timmerman's speech. Now someone had thrown the switch on the mikes, for suddenly a boom of noise filled the narrow corridor, people shouting or running, telephones ringing, prayer wheels spinning, drums with the sloppy rhythms of weekend spirit-travellers, strange popping noises I couldn't identify . . . Several people in the gallery screamed, others held their ears. For me, it came like an alarm waking me from a kind of drugged state. Setting down the bag, I pressed my hands against the window, making sure no one could get between me and a clear view.

A voice announced that the closing bell would ring in five minutes. Those of us in the gallery all looked to the balcony with the cage for the bell that started and ended trading, and beside it the chair where the chairman would sit for the ringing. The chair was a wooden effigy of Rebecca Rainbow sitting on a large stone. Her torso and head formed the chair back, her arms stretched forward for arm rests, her lap would give the chairman his seat. From the literature given to visitors I knew that the eyes of the effigy looked directly at Rainbow herself, in her glass coffin, thirty-six feet above the floor.

On the floor no one looked up at the bell at all. They were all working the phones or computers, shouting at each other, running from one place to the next, gesturing with their hands – all but those who had stopped work ahead of time and now were gathered in small clusters, chanting and setting out representation dolls and other equipment for their own enactments before the main event. It struck me suddenly what they were doing – trying to ensure that when the time came for the Choir of Angels to bless a handful of traders, they would insert themselves into the company of the chosen.

I closed my eyes and put my hand over my face, not wanting to see. I felt like some Speaker who could see the whole event ahead of time. Right then I wished that Alison had left me alone that day in Miracle Park. I wished I could go back and change the sequence of events, so that I would not have to stand alone in that crowded room, waiting for a disaster. Someone touched my arm. I turned to see a man in a pale blue suit, holding out a white handkerchief with red stripes. 'Here,' he said, 'are you all right?'

Somehow, all I could think of was that I hadn't met anyone who used handkerchiefs in about twenty years. 'Thanks,' I said, taking hold of it. Before I could say I was fine or that I really hadn't been crying he smiled at me, then turned and moved away again into the crowd. To my amazement I found myself crying after all. As I wiped the cloth against my face, I whispered, 'Thank you. Whoever you are . . . thanks.'

As if someone had turned up a rheostat, the noise shrieked up another level. It took me a moment to realize that while people on the floor were getting in their last licks, everyone in the gallery had turned towards the balcony, where the chairman of the Exchange, dressed in a gold-leaf business suit, had sat down in his Rebecca Rainbow chair with a gloved hand poised over the button that would set off the bell. It was two hours before closing time and I thought how that alone should have persuaded Timmerman that someone was setting him up, that the coven who ran the Exchange would give up two full hours of trading to make room for this outsider's 'enactment of financial renewal'.

The blue finger of the glove came down and the bell sounded, a low gong followed immediately by a wild cawing and screeching of birds, the artbirds calling on the Living World to witness the end of trading. In the gallery, everyone around me applauded; down in the 'snake pit'

(Li Ku Unquenchable Fire's term for the Exchange, on the one occasion she visited it), people kneeled or even fell to the floor, spreading out their arms and fingers to give back the sacred energy of finance built up over the course of the day.

More than I would have thought possible, I wished for Alison beside me. I knew she had to make that final try, those last phone calls. But I just wanted her holding my hand, standing with me, the only two people who knew what Margaret Light-at-the-End-of-the-Tunnel was going to do to those suckers on the floor, all in the sincere yearning to liberate humanity.

Recorded voices mixed in with the continuing cries of the birds, as Timmerman's theme sounded, distorted by the loudspeakers blaring it to the huge room. 'If not now, when? If not here, where? And if not us, who?'

And then Great Brother Alex himself came in, entering through the doors on the side of the Exchange (carved in the shape of a giant mouth), flanked by security agents in wolf masks and bullet-proof vests (as if Timmerman had nothing to fear but bullets) and Timmerman's own mud-covered assistants, a whole group of them this time. Are they all going to burst into flames? I wondered, remembering the stunt in Miracle Park. But this time Timmerman was the star all by himself. The others crouched down, transforming themselves into mounds of dirt, while Timmerman stood above them, wearing, as well as his bird headdress, a multi-layered paper robe, formed, as far as I could see, from a mixture of newsprint and notarized documents. One of the mudpeople must have set a match to the robe, for flames leapt up from below, to the cheers and whistles of the crowd. Timmerman seemed to step out of the thing while it was still burning still upright behind him, like some other identity he were leaving to its own destruction. He was wearing his trademark grey suit now, treated, I assumed, against fire, as were the mask and any exposed skin. I thought, so this is how they got you, you stupid bastard. You just couldn't resist putting on a show.

The burn sacrifice had taken place in the centre of the floor and the crowd, with people just about climbing each other's backs for a better view. Now, however, the wolfmen escorted Timmerman to a wooden platform towards the side, where he could stand above everybody. Microphones waited for his speech.

But first . . .

Just as in Miracle Park, they came out of the crowd, this time wearing the yellow blazers of brokers. Albert Comfort the Children 6 and Jeannette Benevolent Fire 31. And if the people in the park had fought each other to get closer, this crowd acted like rival hives of bees fighting over the carcass of some dead bull. You might have thought they could kill each other and expect the Benign Ones to reward them for their sincerity and dedication. Those who had given up trading to do enactments now waved the dolls or other tools they'd used. The others just shoved. Engrossed in their struggles, they didn't even stop to call out the Formula. The people around me in the gallery did it for them.

While the other visitors shouted their gratitude, I stood there, my hands tight on the railing, my eyes fixed on the Happy Twins themselves. How? I wondered. How were they going to do it? What would they do to make this event, this 'liberation' so much greater than all the others? Would they just count on the ferocity of the audience itself, or would they do something special to increase the voltage of their blessing?

It took me a moment to realize that the Twins were not actually touching anyone, but instead were just standing there, one on either side of Timmerman, while the wolf agents kept back the traders. They were going to have to do something else, the old touching wasn't going to be enough, they couldn't count on the TV cameras simply picking up the liberation of a few people, they wanted to reach everybody who was there, really send out a message. And the world had to see. That was the point. Looking down at the floor, I noticed that the TV cameras from the networks were unmanned, set up on signal-controlled rotating platforms. Had Channing warned them, told the news people, 'Don't put your crews on the floor, you'll do better with cameras you can control from far away'?

TV. Videos. The small screens that came out on their insect arms from the larger monitors above the trading posts – they reached down to a height where anyone could touch them. That's it, I thought. That's how they can reach all of them, give them all the full dose without having to touch them. The Twins were holding microphones and whispering or maybe singing, crooning, into them. It was such a low hum, almost like a modulated feedback, except that I could feel it all through my spine, a tiny crackling at every nerve ending. All around me, the people in the gallery were gasping, or laughing, hugging each other in astonishment, or closing their eyes to sway from side to side.

Down on the floor, no one had shut their eyes. Instead they were grabbing at the videos, jumping up against them, kissing them. Some of them had cut themselves on the sharp corners of the monitors, but they weren't feeling any pain. They just laughed and rubbed the blood on the screens, all over their clothes and faces, smearing it on the other people who were jumping up alongside them.

At last, I think, Timmerman was starting to understand what they were doing to him. For he was trying to speak, to give out his pronouncements, the revelations of scandal which he had planned as the main event, the denunciation of Arthur Channing and the bankers who'd systematically been robbing the American economy. Only no one was listening. They were all shouting and laughing, you could hardly hear Brother Alex at all, despite the giant loudspeakers hanging from the latticework of computer cables. I could see a kind of desperation in his body as

he leaned forward, struggling for the attention of people
who were beginning to touch, or lick, everything in sight
– the phones, the desks, scraps of paper, any equipment
they could rub against, or grab hold of, or climb up to
slide their bodies on the smooth surfaces, the hard edges
and corners.

Timmerman had to understand, I thought. He had to
see finally what Alison and I had been trying to tell him.
He could give his speech, he could fire his cannons against
Arthur Channing and anyone else, he could submit the
text, even the proof, to all the papers and television. But
no one was listening. No one would listen ever again. All
of Timmerman's carefully researched findings of corruption and conspiracy in the national banking system would
go unheard, drowned out in the astonishment and horror
of Margaret Light-at-the-End-of-the-Tunnel 23's distorted
vision of human liberation.

Here on the visitors' gallery the blessing song was
beginning to penetrate us. We couldn't touch the videos
like the people on the floor. We could only hear a
secondary transmission of the Choir of Angels. But it
was enough to bring some people rubbing up against
the glass barrier, even pounding on it, as if they would
smash through and leap down to where they could get
the undiluted blessing. Others caressed each other or
else the loudspeakers carrying up the noise from the
trading floor.

Somebody – some guy in a baseball jacket – began to
caress my shoulder. I shoved him, or maybe hit him,
much harder than I intended as I shouted, 'Get away
from me!' A woman about my own age, in a leather
jacket hung with about a hundred tiny dolls, told me,
'That was incredible' as she tried to rub up against me.
I did my best to control myself as I pushed her away. I
wished I could shout something at them that would wake
them up, something like, 'Don't let them do this to you!'
but I knew it was no use.

And down below, in the pit, Timmerman was realizing the same thing. The wolfmen and the mud people were gone, melted into the mob, but no one was bothering Timmerman. He was standing on his makeshift podium, the microphone still in his hand, but now forgotten as he looked from side to side. Before him, his Friends were still singing in their strange needle-thin voices. Timmerman looked like he wanted to stop them yet didn't dare. Or know how.

The broadcast cameras, which had been trained on Timmerman, had all turned now, panning the floor or focusing on some particular person or group. A lot of people had stripped off their clothes, or torn them, some leaving only shredded rags, though curiously the clerks, brokers, reporters and pages had mostly kept on their red, yellow, blue and turquoise jackets. And curiously, there was very little actual screwing going on, as if that would only narrow people's choices and how could they stand to restrict themselves? They were sliding up and down each other's bodies or even rubbing along the floor, they were climbing the insect arms to slam up against the much larger monitors which formed the insect bodies, laughing as they fell off against the floor, the counter, other bodies.

Just as in Miracle Park, I could see that three-year-old innocence in the way people moved against each other and every object they could reach. They were laughing all the time, even when they were moaning or shouting. Someone who had cut himself, probably on a monitor, lay twisting on the floor, offering his blood to whoever desired it. A whole pack of people kneeled or crouched over his body, while others tried to rub against him, but none of them looked at all aggressive or predatory. Just children playing.

Was I wrong? Even if Timmerman would suffer, would no one else get hurt? Was I just a hypocrite? Hadn't I just spent the night with a woman old enough to be, well, not my mother, but at least my aunt? Near me, the man who

had grabbed me was kissing the woman in the doll jacket.
Why shouldn't they do that? I felt suddenly like one of
those people who stand on street corners wearing three
overcoats and shouting about purifying the Revolution of
'lust and concupiscence' whatever that is.

I shook my head, forcing myself to remember what
Alison had told me about her friend Jack, or the other
people, cut or trampled. To remember Joan. And yet,
something in me kept insisting that I was the one who
was wrong, or twisted, that I couldn't just join in with
everybody else. Maybe what happened to Joan was my
fault. If I hadn't rejected her that night we could have
broken through the barriers that make love run down,
that make orgasms dwindle to a flicker which blows out
at the slightest distraction. We could have invited Harry,
Alison, anyone we wanted, to feast with us, eating the
food Margaret Tunnel Light was offering us. Instead, Joan
ended up in the hospital. And here I was again, refusing,
refusing.

A prickliness seized my skin, a jabbing all over my body
that both hurt and excited me. I could see everything
happening on the floor, small details in different places,
all at the same time. At one trading station, people were
pulling the machines apart, ripping the phones out and
rubbing the electronic pieces all over their bodies, cutting
themselves or burning their skin. Two women stood in
torn clothes, taking turns clawing each other up and
down their bodies, using a silver hand with the fingers
extended.

I *was* right, I told myself. This is what I knew would
happen. Me and Arthur Channing. What we knew that
Margaret Tunnel Light didn't. But I couldn't make myself
move or do anything, I just stood and watched. Watched
as people grabbed the ceremonial oversized pens, the
black lacquer and gold ones used for signing contracts,
and jammed them into every hole in their bodies, or else
stabbed themselves and each other with the gold points,

injecting sanctified traders' ink into their blood. Watched
as people began biting each other, as five pages in their
turquoise jackets took out ceremonial scarring knives and
began drawing patterns on an elderly man who wept as he
urinated in their faces. Someone climbed up one of the
cable poles, possibly to try and reach the artbirds, or even
Rebecca Rainbow herself. When he fell and broke his leg,
a man and woman siezed hold of his leg and began twisting
it, as if to snap it right off. When it wouldn't come loose
they abandoned him to join a group who were rubbing
themselves in some play money someone had pulled from
behind a desk. Soon, I knew, people wouldn't stop, not
until they were tearing each other's bodies and ripping out
their insides to rub all over faces without skin or eyes. I
knew this, I could see it as if it was already happening.
But I couldn't make myself move, not even to get myself
out of danger.

Protection, I thought. *Now.* All the things in my bag
that Annie-O had given me. I needed to layer myself or
it would swallow me. But instead of emptying out the bag
I just held it tightly against my body, as if the objects
themselves could save me without having to commit myself
to doing anything with them.

A voice said, 'Nothing can harm you. I have given you
my protection.' I didn't even bother looking around me or
at the loudspeakers. I just scanned the floor. It took me
a moment to find her. She was standing on the podium,
the platform where Timmerman had tried speaking. He
was gone now. And on the platform, between the Twins,
she stood there, serene in her black clothes, her harsh
makeup.

'You don't understand,' I said. 'I don't want you
protecting me.' I gripped the bag even tighter. The rocks
inside pressed into my chest.

My Friend looked up from the floor at me. 'Are you
ready to join them?'

'No!' I shouted at the window. The Being turned,

walked away through the crowds. 'What's the matter with you?' I said. 'Can't you understand you're hurting them? They can't eat what you're feeding them.'

I couldn't see her, but the voice told me, 'They do what they need to do.'

'You've got to take it back,' I called. '*Please*. You're just doing what Channing wanted you to do. Why can't you understand that? *You're hurting Alexander.*'

'No,' she said. 'Alexander is safe. He has left the room and no one is harming him.'

'You're harming him. You're destroying his career.' No answer. 'Don't let them do this!' I yelled, but she was gone. And down on the floor, the Twins remained, singing without mikes now, just their hands cupped in front of their mouths.

I didn't dare look around me. It wasn't as strong here, but I still could hear choking laughter, people slammed against the glass, others thrown on the floor. The floor was slippery and it smelled. 'Ellen,' a voice called to me. I didn't move, just stood with my head pressed against the window. I'd closed my eyes. 'Ellen,' the voice said again, as a hand grabbed my shoulder.

I swung the bag around as hard as I could, knocking the woman down onto a pile of shifting bodies.

Then I saw her, or maybe just part of her, like seeing an arm buried under a landslide. I don't know any more, I can't remember precisely what I saw. 'Alison!' I cried, and reached down for her arm before they could suck her away from me. The people around her were one body, they were all mouth, and they wanted to swallow her. But I got her loose, jerking her to her feet with one hand, because I knew I couldn't let go of the bag, it would vanish, Margaret Tunnel Light would steal it away from me.

'Ellen,' she called once again and held on to me, trying to squeeze me into her body, as if she could absorb me directly into her skin. 'I tried to stop it,' she said. 'I called everyone I knew. I told them everything, I begged them, just for a delay, just a couple of days, even a few hours if I could just talk to Timmerman. Ellen, they wouldn't listen. They wouldn't listen to anything. I felt like such an idiot. They can't *think*. They can't see it when I explain it to them. They can only see that she's Benign, and how could a Benign One cause any harm? I explained it to them and they just wouldn't listen.'

'I know,' I said. I was holding her, stroking her and touching her back, her shoulders, her hair. 'It's like she's bitten them. Or injected some kind of narcotic into them.'

Alison kissed me, on the cheek, the neck, below my ear, my collar bone. Suddenly she made a noise, a grunt or a scream, and it took me a moment to realize she was staring through the window at the trading floor for the first time.

'It's getting worse,' I told her, and held her tightly, stroking her body the whole time I was talking – the two things, the talking and touching, unconnected, as if different people were doing them. 'It just keeps getting worse and worse, and nobody can stop it. They're already clawing at each other, at everything they can reach. They're not going to stop. I thought it was harmless, but it isn't, it's not.' I was kissing her now, kissing and then stopping to talk, back and forth, unable to stop either action. 'She said we're protected, you and I. Like she's cast some Goddamn blanket over us.'

Alison was moving up and down my body, making herself liquid as she spread her fingers wide and slithered them down my arms, my breasts, slamming her thighs into mine, pushing me up against the railing. 'She said she'd protect us. All the stuff I brought, the stuff from Annie—' I realized suddenly that I'd dropped the bag. I knew I should look for it, but I couldn't. I couldn't stop touching Alison. I didn't need it, I told myself. Margaret Tunnel Light would protect us.

Alison was touching my breasts through my clothes,

rubbing my nipples with the flattened palms of her hands. At the same time, she kept grimacing, crunching her face, as if in pain. Several times she opened her mouth, with no sound, until finally she burst out, 'That goddamn *music.*' For the first time since Alison had shown up, I heard the song, the shrill whine of the Choir of Angels.

7

'It's all right,' I told her, only vaguely conscious of how absurd the statement was. I was kissing her, sliding down and rubbing against her. I knew I should take her away, cover her ears, but all I could do was kiss them, biting her ears and then all over her face while I pushed her back against the railing. Near me, someone was vomiting convulsively while someone else squatted underneath him.

I started pulling at Alison's clothes, unable to remember how they came off and getting lost in the fabric, or scraping the zipper of her windbreaker across my tongue and then my breasts. Alison was doing something, she was crying for some reason. I wanted to lick the tears for the salt, but couldn't move my mouth from her clothes, her skin, where they met . . .

Someone slammed against me. A woman of about seventy was trying to get at the window, through the window, trying to reach the song. There were children hanging on her, a very young boy and girl literally holding on to her arms, which she waved about as she butted her head against the plate glass, so that the children almost flapped in the air like flags.

Get out of here, I thought. We had to get out of there. But my bag was gone. I needed my bag from Annie-O. 'Help me find my bag!' I shouted at Alison, who began pushing people aside to reach the floor, where people were rolling around or else touching and hitting each other. Somehow we found it, two women had it, they were rubbing the leather against their bodies, laughing as they pushed it up against their breasts from below. Now they were opening it, taking out one rock, or cord, or fabric at a time in order to taste it or rub it in their hair. I thought Alison and I would have to fight them for it, but when we pushed them aside they laughed and immediately took to pushing each other and then whoever was next to them, laughing and pushing and then kicking as hard as they could.

I grabbed a dress I'd gotten from Annie. 'Put this on,' I ordered Alison. 'Over your clothes.' I didn't dare undress or let Alison expose any more of her skin. The sight of it burned, I could see it crackling, small licks of flame flaring on her face and arms. The dress was a 'relic' charged with the energy of outlaw enactments Annie and her cross-sisters had done in caves, computer centres and anonymous hotel rooms. While Alison put it on, I chose my own relic, a strand of heavy blue beads on a red silk cord. Annie and her relics had power because of who Annie was, and because of the blessing work she and her women had done over decades. But she had special power for Alison and me because she'd done everything without the help of the SDA or Bright Beings.

There were pots of red mud in each bag, one clay jar for each of us to smear on our faces, necks and hands. It made me think of Timmerman and his mud-covered escorts, but it cooled me and weighed me down, as if it covered my whole body, turning me into one of those cave statues, all breasts and hips, you sometimes see in museums for precursors of the Revolution.

The bag contained things I didn't understand – a can opener, a railway ticket from England, torn pieces of what looked like a medical report, a gold-headed hammer – and other things that made a little more sense, like a cracked pomegranate, a comb in the shape of a bird with outstretched wings, a mirror set into a small wooden bowl, a tiny bow and arrow, and a claw from some animal. Most important was a small leather pouch filled with folded photographs and dirt. Annie's soul memories. I'd asked her why she was taking such a chance lending me these things and all she would do was put on her tough voice and tell me, 'Let's just say I don't like Devoted Ones. Okay?' adding, 'Anyway, us humans got to stick together.'

The bulk of the bag was in rocks, which, like the mud Annie had brought back from enactments done in wilderness power places around the world. Alison started to take them out, but I raised my heavy mud hand to stop her. I pointed to the ground, then waved my hand, signalling 'Not here'. She nodded and I led her through the thick press of people, moving ponderously, mudpeople through a world of fire.

Moving through the flashes of ecstasy exploding all around us, I suddenly felt like an enemy of the Revolution, of human freedom – a thief, a traitor, someone who would be hated throughout history for bringing history back from the dead. Desire and the endless body had killed history and now Alison and I were going to murder desire, cover it with mud.

All around us people had abandoned their bodies to live forever in the body of smells, of faceless tongues and teeth, of skin spread so wide it became invisible. Others were sending roots down through the cracked floors, down through the Manhattan granite, lines from their penises and vaginas to draw up the juices of the Earth, while Alison and I became drier and drier, our dead mud bodies about to wither into dust.

I didn't even realize I was turning back until Alison gripped my arm. She pulled me along like some lost child, at whatever cost to herself, past the souvenir stands where people were shoving plaster models of Rebecca Rainbow into their groins, or jabbing themselves with gold leather openers, or masturbating each other with silver statues of the bulls and bears slaughtered by Rainbow's followers on the day the Founder reopened the Stock Exchange. We moved past the video question and answer machines, now torn from their slots, until finally I smashed up against a wall and realized there was nobody there, we'd come around the corner to the row of elevators connecting the gallery and the street and had tumbled into silence.

Without a word we set out the stones from the bag. They were small mostly, about palm size, and marked with lines across their softly curved female surfaces. We set them in a loose circle, then filled the circle with Annie's emblems of humanity. In the centre we made a small fire, not of flash powder, but only pieces of paper, newsprint, letters, even junk mail and old receipts or cancelled cheques, all of it mixed with flowers and weeds plucked from Miracle Park. With the fire some of the weight lifted off me.

I took out a silver jar from the bottom of the bag. The jar held dirt, and as I held it up I thought I could see Alison smile underneath her mud mask. The two of us had made this particular relic together, travelling out to the Forbidden Beach for sand, then setting it out on the floor of my apartment where we squatted down and pissed on it until we could form a brown paste.

Alison and I clapped our hands together to shake off some of the mud. It was the first time either of us had made a sound and I found myself crying at the discovery that sound was still possible, even without the Song of the Blessed. The next part was the hardest, for it meant tempting ourselves with a leap into Tunnel Light's world. We each reached into the jar with our left hands, while unbuttoning each other's blouses with our right.

We smeared the paste on each other's breasts, bellies, thighs and finally genitals. Instead of the hurricane I'd feared, a softness settled over us. 'I love you,' I said, and Alison repeated it back at me, as the heated mud on our faces cracked and fell in chunks onto the edge of the fire. We reached across for each other's hands, rocking on our heels slightly, hearing the distant hum of terror and desire.

'Ready?' Alison said.

'I hope so.'

For the past two days, while Alison had battled on the telephone, I had studied how to do a Summoning – the formulas, the props, the preparations. In the end, I had had to discard everything. Whoever had done the original research and development, it all belonged now to the SDA. Finally, I remembered Adrienne Birth-of-Beauty's Fifteenth Proposition – 'There are no rules except discovery. There is no tradition except invention.'

I stripped off what remained of my clothes. 'Paint me?' I said. Alison spat into the ashes from the fire, then scooped up a small amount to mix into the paste with more spit. She held up her left forefinger and kissed it, looking at me as we both remembered how that finger had lifted my whole body early in the morning, before she'd gotten back on the phones and I'd left her to go to the disaster.

Eyes closed, I let her paint an enactment face on me, the lines and concentric circles a summary of both our lives – initiation markings, family scar designs we'd shown each other, words of power from our deep journeys, images from the screen we'd painted on our first night together. When she'd finished, I reached into my bag for the amulet the SDA had given me as well as a small glass pot containing dried menstrual blood from my first period. With Annie's hammer I smashed the amulet, then used the pieces to form a small circle inside the larger one. Using the powdered blood my left middle finger drew two stick figures, one outside the outer circle, the other in the centre, with a line running between them.

When we'd planned the Summoning, Alison and I had spent half an hour deciding what designation we should use for our target. What name would reach her? Finally, Alison convinced me that for a Bright Being, as for humanity, rcality consisted of whatever identity she was inhabiting right now.

My finger wrote Margaret Tunnel Light's name in menstrual blood and spit. 'Blessed Being,' I said, 'we ask your entry into this circle of our lives. We thank you now and forever for all the gifts you have given us and will give us.' I said it three times.

There was nothing else to do. If I'd brought flash powder I could have rounded off the ceremonial part, but we'd decided to stay with our own tools. And so we waited, just squatting, while I thought of the people below, of Paul, of Alison and me.

Behind me an elevator door opened. When I turned around Margaret Light-at-the-End-of-the-Tunnel 23 was walking towards me.

'It's time,' she said. 'You understand. I'm pleased that you have called me.' The elevator door behind her stayed open.

I stood up. 'No,' I said. 'We understand that what you are doing must stop.'

She smiled, allowing her teeth to flare for an instant, overwhelming the fluorescent lights of the hallway. 'Do you think you can compel me?' she asked. 'With your Summoning?' I said nothing. 'I came to show you,' Margaret Tunnel Light said. 'To show you how much I respect you and love you.'

'You have to stop,' I told her. 'I know you want to give us something. And you think it's good for us. But we can't – we're not ready for it.'

She ignored me. 'I have let you taste the food I can give you. The two of you together. And I have let you go so that you will know that I love you and will never harm you.'

'You just don't understand what you're doing to them. Or why. You've been tricked. Used by human beings who don't care about anything except destroying Alexander Timmerman.'

'I've told you before,' she said. 'Human schemes do not interest me. But I will never harm Alexander.'

'If you destroy his cause you destroy him. You've got to understand that. What you're doing today is destroying everything he cares about. Everything he loves.'

She looked very young suddenly, with her deep black-ringed eyes, her short hair. 'Child,' she said. 'I cannot harm him. Or any human being. I simply cannot. The nature of my nature is devotion.'

'No!' I shouted at her. Alison touched my arm, but I pushed her away. 'You're not a Devoted One. You're Malignant. You killed my cousin. Paul Cabot. *Paul Cabot.* You *killed* him. Set your snakes on him.'

She said, 'Something has disturbed you. There are enemies. Let me inside and I will free you.'

I took a step backwards and spit on the floor. My left hand slashed at the air. 'I forbid you to enter me.'

'Why do you insist on this? I've never hurt you. I've never touched any Paul Cabot.'

'Your name,' I said, 'is Lisa Black Dust 7.'

'You know very well my designation.'

'Now. Now you're Margaret Light-at-the-End-of-the-Tunnel 23. But you were Lisa Black Dust 7 first. You ran a service in an office building. An agency for Malignant Ones who worked for the government. Paul worked there. In that building. And you ate him. Why won't you remember?'

She shook her head. 'No. This is your sickness. False stories about me will not help you, Ellen.'

Rubbing my hands together, I removed as much as I could of the paint and paste, then wiped the marks from my face. The Being said, 'What are you doing?' When I glanced at Alison she was looking at me with narrowed eyes, concentrating. She nodded slightly and I realized once again how much I loved her.

'I'm exposing myself,' I said to Tunnel Light. 'Can you read humans? Can you tell when a human is telling the truth? When a human knows the truth?' I opened my arms. 'I want you to read me.'

She stepped close to look at my face. When she touched my cheek, I forced myself not to jump back. Her fingers felt – ordinary. Soft, and a little cold. She moved her fingers around my cheeks, my ears, underneath my jaw, and then held them for a while on the side of my neck.

She dropped her arms finally and stepped back. 'I don't understand,' she said. 'I know my purpose. I know my function.'

'They brought you back. To serve *their* purpose. Arthur Channing and his crooked friends who didn't want Alexander Timmerman investigating the banking system. They couldn't use a Malignant One since Timmerman would just protect himself. So they let you change to Benign and sent you in to destroy him, his organization. That was your real purpose.'

She shook her head. She looked like a child, scared and confused. 'But if I still can help? What does it matter if a human scheme brought me here? My purpose remains true. Why should—'

Down the hall an elevator door had opened and now three men in tubular masks were moving towards us. Two of the men held guns, the third carried a spray gun attached by hose to a heavy canister covered in markings and tied round with sanctified nylon cord hung with beads. Demon breaker.

One of the men said, 'Ellen Pierson, Alison Birkett, you're under arrest. Turn around and face the wall.'

Tunnel Light said, 'These women are under my protection. I cannot allow —'

The agent in the middle was raising the nozzle. 'Ferocious One,' he said, 'I beg you—'

I shoved Tunnel Light aside before he could spray her. Grabbing Alison's hand, I pushed the Being into the elevator she'd left open behind her. 'Paul!' I shouted. 'Close the door. *Hurry.*' I screamed as a bullet hit the wall behind us and ricocheted around the chamber. But then the door was closed and we were moving downwards. 'Paul,' I said. 'Take us between floors. And disable the other elevators.'

I turned Maggie Tunnel Light to face the steel column at the front of the elevator. Confused, she didn't resist. 'Look,' I said. 'This is what you did to him. You killed him. And then the government and the Bright Beings stuck him here, in elevators.'

Whether the others saw or not, I don't know – I've never asked Alison – but to me, Paul's face appeared in the air at the top of the column, in front of the jewels and hair. He looked just as I remembered him from that last day, only – not so scared, more peaceful. 'I love you,' I whispered, but I knew I couldn't stay looking at him. Right now, our Friend had to get my attention.

She was changing, moving in and out of a different form, taller, with a fuller body. *Lisa Black Dust 7*, I thought. *She's changing back to the Ferocious One.* I opened my mouth to tell Paul to get us out of there, take us downstairs, but I couldn't speak. I couldn't even lift my arm to signal him. Next to me, Alison was pressed back against the wall, struggling against whatever invisible arm held her there.

The Being leaned forward with her mouth open, smiling like a delighted five year old. 'Ellen Pierson,' she said, as if thrilled to see me again. 'Are you ready for me to eat you?'

I backed away, reaching for Alison.

And then Alison and I fell down as Black Dust 7 vanished, taking the pressure with her. Margaret Tunnel Light stood there again, weeping in the dim light of the elevator. 'I don't understand,' she said. 'I just wanted to feed you. That's all. I just wanted to feed you.'

Exhausted finally, I couldn't answer, just sat there watching her cry. Alison stood up and walked to her. 'We can't take your food,' she said. I don't think I'd ever heard such kindness in her voice, not even when she was holding me after Paul's death. 'Humans can only feed each other. I know you tried, but it's just part of our nature. We long for you to help us and feed us, but in the end our love for each other is the only food we can eat. I'm sorry. Really. I wish it was different. For all of us as well as for you.'

Margaret Light-At-The-End-Of-Tunnel 23 dropped her head. She began to rock back and forth, with her arms wrapped around her chest. I stood up and took Alison's hand.

The Being straightened. She closed her eyes a moment, then opened them again, her face calm. Turning to me, she said, 'Please ask your cousin to take us downstairs.'

I glanced at Alison who nodded. 'Paul,' I said. The elevator moved. When we touched the ground floor, Tunnel Light said, 'Bury your faces in your bodies.' It took us a moment to realize what she meant, but when the door opened Alison and I had safely pressed our eyes into each other's shoulders as a flash of light filled the corridor. When we stepped out of the elevator five or six men and women were on the ground, groaning or pulling off their tube masks to press their hands against their eyes. Ignoring them, we followed Tunnel Light, who had already moved through the lobby and onto the trading floor.

You've probably seen something of what Alison and I found when we entered that room. For those who didn't catch it on live television, the news programmes made sure to run the tapes several hundred times (with men in suits giving sombre warnings beforehand about the disturbing footage). But even if you saw the unedited live version, the bleeding bodies, the vomit and shit, the torn arms and ripped-open chests, the people naked or wearing layers of clothes, the people sitting and staring, the ones wandering or falling down, the cut and the dead, the ones lying face down on the floor, and all around them the smashed computers, the ripped-out wires and telephones, even if you saw all of it, the screen could never show what it was like to step into it. To climb over the bodies and feel limp hands brush against our legs, to step between the dead and the staring, watching out for live wires and glass and pieces of bodies. And the silence, the absence of any human noise, not even moans or weeping, so that the only things we could hear were the whisper of the cameras and the slight background hum of the loudspeakers, along with the cheerful whistle of the artbirds, still fluttering around Rebecca Rainbow's impassive body. And the smell, that battering ram hit of emptied-out bodies, of come and blood and vomit, all mingled with burnt rubber and plastic, overlaid at the same time with a cloud of perfume, a smell of flowers as delicate as the song of the birds.

We didn't go very far into the room. Harry and Glorybe told us later that one of the cameras focused on us for just a moment, but I never saw it on any of the broadcasts (though to be fair, I watched very few of them). We picked our way through the bodies for a few yards until we just stopped, holding hands and staring all around.

The Happy Twins were gone, along with Timmerman and his mudpeople. But Margaret 23 was there, in the middle of the room. She turned and saw us. 'Go home,' she said. 'This is finished.'

Instead of leaving, Alison and I turned to each other and without any discussion we placed our left hands over each other's hearts and said, in slow rhythm, 'The Blessing of the Saved. Open your heart to the Sun. Open your eyes to the Sky. Open your ears to the Sea. Deep love to the round Earth who has given us bodies. Deep love to the dead stars for their dust and their light. Deep love to our mothers and our fathers, for the gene patterns of our souls. Deep love to our mothers, for the blood homes of our first growth. We bless each other for the entrances into our bodies. We are women of dirt. We are women of bone. We are women of mucus. We are women of light.

We are women of words. We are saved. We are blessed. We are saved.'

Our hands dropped to our sides, then once more found each other and we stepped through the bodies broken by ecstasy into each other's arms.

8

The lobby of Paul's old office building looked pretty much like it had on that last day, thirteen years ago, the dark wood panels, the brass knobs and fittings, the tiles with their soft colours filling the floor. For a while, I just stood there, staring down at the mosaic of the Army of the Saints, as if the Founders somehow could liberate me the way they'd liberated New Chicago. Finally, I just shrugged and stepped up to the row of elevators.

On the way over, I'd wondered if I'd remember which one it was. Now, there was no question in my mind. Not that it mattered, for before I could even press the button the correct door slid open. He was waiting for me. I took a look around to make sure no one was following me, but it was Saturday and the lobby was empty save for a few tourists who just wanted to photograph the floor. As soon as I stepped inside, the door slid shut behind me.

'Hello, Paul,' I said. The steel column shone for a moment and I ran my hand along it. It was a pretty nice one, not quite so extravagant as the one in the Stock Exchange, but polished, with real hair or a decent imitation. 'Maybe we should go somewhere,' I said. The elevator rose so smoothly I could hardly detect the movement or just when it stopped, but I assumed we were between floors.

'Look,' I said, 'I needed . . . I wanted to talk with you. I'm sorry. For staying away so long. It's just . . . it's just that it's taken me a long time to understand some things.' I shook my head, trying to get all my thoughts into the right order. 'I guess I avoided seeing you – coming here – or any of your other places – I just couldn't deal with it. I didn't want to think about it. But then – well, Alison came back. But you know that. If you can recognize me, you can probably recognize her as well.'

I stopped for a moment, as if he might want to reply, then realized how impossible that was and smiled. It was hard talking to someone who couldn't answer, or show any recognition at all. But I still had to say it. 'You know, I tried really hard to blame Alison. And if not her, then me. Or the government. Or the Living World. But I kept leaving someone out. You.

'Shit. I wish I could hug you. What I'm trying to say is, I wanted to see you as a victim. But I understand now, Paul. No one forced you into this elevator. You saw the snakes as clearly as I did. You were making a choice. Lisa Black Dust 7 had given you a taste of something and you decided you just didn't want to give it up. Oh, Paul.' I half raised my arms, as if I really would wrap them around that steel house holding him. But the damn husk was just too thin. Too thin and too hard.

I said, 'I love you, Paul. You made a choice. Desire over safety. I wish you hadn't. But I've just got to accept that you did what you wanted to do. And that's okay. It has to be. I love you.'

Sparks flew off the steel column and just for a second it seemed to double in size, with the jewels on top looking almost like eyes. But then the sparks died and Paul was gone again, leaving only a dull metal tube. 'Goodbye,' I whispered. Maybe, I thought, he'd gone to some other elevator, where someone needed him more than I did. I pressed the button for 'G'; in a moment, the door opened on the lobby.

Outside, I passed an open magazine kiosk with a portable television perched on a stool in the corner.

A crowd of about thirty people stood pressed together, blocking the sidewalk as they tried to get a good view. Though I knew what they were watching I went and joined them, just to see it.

It was the news conference, of course. Alison, Timmerman and Margaret Light-At-The-End-Of-The-Tunnel 23. They were standing in a neat row, Alison in her blue silk suit, Timmerman without his mask, Tunnel Light in the same black outfit she'd worn in the park. Probably it was her skin, with nothing underneath it.

It was Alison's turn to speak. Leaning towards the cluster of microphones, she was explaining the method by which Arthur Channing had manipulated the Devoted Ones. I couldn't hear much. It didn't matter. I just stood and watched her, Alison Birkett, and my body so filled with love, like helium, that I almost expected to float up into the air like Ingrid Burning Snake when she told the story of 'The Empty Daughter'. Instead, a couple of teenage girls pushed me aside, trying to get a clearer view.

Maybe they'll fall in love with her, I thought. Cut out her picture from magazines. Trying not to laugh, I turned from the crowd and headed on home, smiling happily as I thought of Alison's body lying beside me.